UNWRAPPED

Praise for D. Jackson Leigh

Unbridled

"A hot, steamy, erotic romance mystery with edge, exciting twists and turns, great characters and an unforgettable story that I was completely invested in. It was difficult to put the book down and I thoroughly enjoyed the whole experience of reading it!"
—*LESBIReviewed*

Blades of Bluegrass

"Both lead characters, Britt and Teddy, were well developed and likeable. I also really enjoyed the supporting characters, like E.B., and the warm, familiar atmosphere the author managed to create at Story Hill Farm."—*Melina Bickard, Librarian, Waterloo Library (UK)*

Ordinary Is Perfect

"There's something incredibly charming about this small town romance, which features a vet with PTSD and a workaholic marketing guru as a fish out of water in the quiet town. But it's the details of this novel that make it shine."—*Pink Heart Society*

Take a Chance

"I really enjoyed the character dynamic with this book of two very strong independent women who aren't looking for love but fall for the one they already love…The chemistry and dynamic between these two is fantastic and becomes even more intense when their sexual desires take over."—*Les Rêveur*

Dragon Horse War

"Leigh writes with an emotion that she in turn gives to the characters, allowing us insight into their personalities and their very souls. Filled with fantastic imagery and the down-to-earth flaws that are sometimes the characters' greatest strengths, this first *Dragon Horse War* is a story not to be missed. The writing is flawless, the story, breath-taking—and this is only the beginning."—*Lambda Literary Review*

"The premise is original, the fantasy element is gripping but relevant to our times, the characters come to life, and the writing is phenomenal. It's the author's best work to date and I could not put it down."—*Melina Bickard, Librarian, Waterloo Library (UK)*

"Already an accomplished author of many romances, Leigh takes on fantasy and comes up aces...So, even if fantasy isn't quite your thing, you should give this a try. Leigh's backdrop is a world you already recognize with some slight differences, and the characters are marvelous. There's a villain, a love story, and...ah yes, 'thar be dragons.'"—*Out in Print: Queer Book Reviews*

"This book is great for those that like romance with a hint of fantasy and adventure."—*The Lesbrary*

"Skin Walkers" in *Women of the Dark Streets*

"When love persists through many lifetimes, there is always the potential magic of reunion. Climactically resplendent!"—*Rainbow Book Reviews*

Swelter

"I don't think there is a single book D. Jackson Leigh has written that I don't like...I recommend this book if you want a nice romance mixed with a little suspense."—*Kris Johnson, Texas Library Association*

"This book is a great mix of romance, action, angst, and emotional drama...The first half of the book focuses on the budding relationship between the two women, and the gradual revealing of secrets. The second half ramps up the action side of things...There were some good sexy scenes, and also an appropriate amount of angst and introspection by both women as feelings more than just the physical started to surface."—*Rainbow Book Reviews*

Call Me Softly

"*Call Me Softly* is a thrilling and enthralling novel of love, lies, intrigue, and Southern charm."—*Bibliophilic Book Blog*

Touch Me Gently

"D. Jackson Leigh understands the value of branding, and delivers more of the familiar and welcome story elements that set her novels apart from other authors in the romance genre."—*Rainbow Reader*

Every Second Counts

"Her prose is clean, lean, and mean—elegantly descriptive."—*Out in Print: Queer Book Reviews*

Riding Passion

"The sex was always hot and the relationships were realistic, each with their difficulties. The technical writing style was impeccable, ranging from poetic to more straightforward and simple. The entire anthology was a demonstration of Leigh's considerable abilities."—*2015 Rainbow Awards*

By the Author

Romance

Call Me Softly

Touch Me Gently

Hold Me Forever

Swelter

Take a Chance

Ordinary Is Perfect

Blades of Bluegrass

Unbridled

Forever Comes in Threes

Here for You

When Tomorrow Comes

Unwrapped

Cherokee Falls Series

Bareback

Long Shot

Every Second Counts

Dragon Horse War Trilogy

The Calling

Tracker and the Spy

Seer and the Shield

Short story collection

Riding Passion

Visit us at www.boldstrokesbooks.com

UNWRAPPED

by

D. Jackson Leigh

2024

UNWRAPPED

ISBN 13: 978-1-63679-667-3

This Trade Paperback Original Is Published By
Bold Strokes Books, Inc.
P.O. Box 249
Valley Falls, NY 12185

First Edition: November 2024

CREDITS
EDITOR: SHELLEY THRASHER
PRODUCTION DESIGN: STACIA SEAMAN
COVER DESIGN BY INKSPIRAL DESIGN

Acknowledgments

As always, I have to thank my very excellent editor, Dr. Shelley Thrasher, and the entire Bold Strokes Books crew for their expertise and support.

I owe a very special thanks to my friend Paige Braddock for letting me use her book *Jane's World: The Case of the Mail Order Bride* in my story. While my story is fiction, her book is real, available at www.boldstrokesbooks.com and most other book outlets. My great-nephews and great-nieces love her children's books, and she also writes fantastic lesbian romances under the pen name Missouri Vaun. Check her out.

Acknowledgments

CHAPTER ONE

I make bad decisions when I'm naked.

This fact is once again obvious to me since I am naked under the sheet and in a bedroom I don't recognize.

In my defense, I was drunk last night and stinging from Lisa Langston's brush-off at her birthday-bash afterparty. Lisa and I are starring in the hit television show *Judge and Jury*, which has already been renewed for a sixth season. Well, Lisa's the star, and I'm a supporting actor. Our characters are law colleagues with lots of hints of lesbian attraction. In real life, I'm her lesbian affair of the month—only I'm blindsided by the now-obvious "of the month" part.

Lisa's lesbianism is an open secret only among the gay community and a certain segment of showbiz people, so I understood when she came to her birthday party with the handsome male star of another popular television show on her arm. Gossip columnists, network executives, and other showbiz people were invited to that big blowout, and for business reasons it is important she adhere to the pretense of being straight.

But I didn't understand when she appeared at the lesbians-only afterparty bash with one of Hollywood's hottest female movie actors and treated me like any other lesbian in the room. We'd made mad, passionate love the night before…in her bed… topping off several months of hot, sex-filled days and nights. So you can see why I believed I was more than another flavor of the month. Hell, I was ready to profess my undying love for her, but she made it clear I'd reached my expiration date.

I roll over and groan when sunlight hits my face. My eyes are burning, my head is pounding, and my mouth is a desert. I shield my eyes to take in the unfamiliar bedroom and my clothes strewn across the hardwood floor leading up to the bed. Shit. Fuzzy recollections of the previous night begin to surface—Lisa greeting me at the door of her mansion with the same cheek-kiss she gave every new arrival, then turning to put a deep lip-lock on the famously out-and-proud movie star glued to her side. What the hell?

A party veteran, Lisa adroitly dodged every attempt I made to corner her for an explanation. The more attention Lisa lavished on the film actor, the more I drank and sulked. The last half of the party is a complete blank, and I have no recollection of leaving, which explains why I have no idea whose bedroom floor I very well might throw up on in the next few minutes.

I sit up and swallow through a nauseating wave of dizziness. My head throbs like an old Tarzan movie where a whole village of African natives are beating a hundred drums to foreshadow something bad is about to happen. Gingerly sliding from the bed, I make another bad decision, which I blame on still being naked, by bending down to retrieve my underwear from the floor. Nearly pitching headfirst when my head explodes with pain, I regain my balance by grabbing the bedpost.

Someone is talking in the next room. Damn. I was hoping last night's conquest had gone out for bagels or something so I could dress, call an Uber, and leave before she returned. What am I thinking? This isn't New York City. It's California. You don't walk a few blocks away to get bagels. You call to have them delivered.

Urgency forces me to focus. Okay. I can do this. Squatting without bending over allows me to retrieve the rest of my clothing without tossing my cookies, so I duck into the adjoining bathroom to dress, splash water on my face, and rinse my mouth.

A quick check of the medicine cabinet produces ibuprofen, and I drink from the faucet to wash several down. Now to face the music or, rather, my host. I creep to the bedroom door and listen.

"Hell, no. This is no AI fake. I plead the Fifth on how I got the footage at the party, but I shot that video of Lisa Langston with her tongue halfway down the throat of Charleigh Long while Charleigh is feeling her up. But the money video is Davis Hart ranting about how she's been fucking Lisa for a couple of months, then got the cold shoulder at the birthday bash. I filmed that right here in my apartment."

I peek around the door frame to see a very attractive blonde pacing the length of her garden apartment with her cell phone held to her ear and inwardly groan. What did I say the night before?

"And…wait for it…I have footage of her getting naked and luring me into bed. The lesbians are going to drool over that. I'm holding it back to post later to keep my hits up."

If I slept with this gorgeous woman, why can't I remember?

"What? No! I didn't sleep with her. Are you kidding? I like dick with a man attached to it. It didn't keep her from trying, though."

I rub my temples and try to ignore the foreboding that's making me want to shake myself and wake up from this nightmare.

"She was pretty drunk but consented on camera to being videoed." A pause while she listens to the person on the other end of the call. "No kidding. I asked if she minded if I left the video on, and she said, 'Whatever turns you on, baby.'"

God damn it. I'm going to snatch that phone from her and delete that video before I leave. I crouch slightly and prepare to spring into action.

"I'm not an idiot. It's already uploaded to two of my clouds in case she tries to delete it from my phone when she wakes up."

Shit. What should I do now? My head is so fuzzy. I need to get out of here and think. If she'll just stop pacing and turn her back to my exit path, maybe I can escape unnoticed.

"Are you crazy? I'm not going to sell this stuff to one of those entertainment shows or gossip rags," she says.

Whew. I hold my hand to my stuttering heart. Maybe I should stick around and play nice. Hell. I'll even sleep with her again. No, wait. She said she didn't sleep with me. My brain is a complete blank after carrying a bottle of Lisa's best single-malt scotch out to the pool to drown my insecurity. I shake my head, hoping to dislodge a memory from the previous night.

"I plan to upload this to my own blog as soon as I edit it a little. In a couple of hours probably. Then I'll post links to it on some of the lesbian websites."

Holy shit. That video could go viral in minutes.

"Then those gossip vultures can pay me to come on their shows and talk about how I got the videos. And they can pay me lots of money to allow them to show the actual ones. So, until I can get the copyright on them, I'm watermarking everything. I'm afraid the kissing video alone will blow up my website. That's why I'm calling you. I need to find out how I can pump it up to handle the millions of hits I'm sure I'll get."

Shit. I need to do something. I clear my throat and step out of the bedroom. She immediately turns to me and smiles.

"Gotta go. She's finally awake."

I quickly decide how to play this scene. After all, I am an actress. I look at her under hooded eyes and treat her to my most sultry smile—something I've practiced countless hours in front of a mirror. Then I lower my voice to a rasping, sexy tone. Maybe she's not as straight as she thinks. I was likely too drunk last night to give her full-on Davis charm. "Hey. I'm disappointed you didn't wake me before you left our bed." I purposely say "our bed" to lure the gossip girl into my seduction. We'll have sex. Then she'll fall asleep, and I'll tiptoe out here to delete the videos on her phone, laptop, and, hopefully, her clouds. After that, I'll sneak out of her apartment, and this whole debacle will fade away.

She smiles at me and sashays over to touch me on the cheek.

I catch her hand and press it against my aching temple, then kiss her palm. "Can I talk you into coming back to bed?" I wrap an arm around her lower back and tug her close, pressing my hips into hers. "Apparently, getting drunk last night didn't keep me from going home with the hottest girl at the party." I kiss her lightly, slowly on the lips, then step back and take her hand to lead her back into the bedroom.

She laughs—a light, delighted titter—and pulls her hand free. "Slow down, Romeo. You obviously don't remember much about last night, because I slept on the sofa." She points to a blanket and pillow on the aforementioned furniture. "You stripped naked after throwing up twice—which was very gross—and crawled into my bed before I could guide you out here to the couch."

I blink, trying again to clear the fog of my memory. "We didn't sleep together?"

The tittering laughter again. "Not that you didn't try, but no. I'm solidly straight. And even though I made that clear last night, you said you didn't care and promised to"—she made air quotes—"rock my world. Then you began to snore like a hibernating bear."

No longer needing to follow my intended script, I scowl. "You took advantage of me. I'm going to call the police."

Again that stupid laugh. I want to wrap my hands around her throat and choke it out of her.

"What's the charge?"

I stumble around in my head for a response. "Kidnapping!"

She rolls her eyes. "I kept an inebriated woman from driving herself home. Am I forcing you to stay here now?" She gestures to the door. "In fact, I'd like for you to leave."

"Not until you delete the videos you made of me when I was incapacitated."

She gives a sarcastic snort. "I didn't drug you. You were self-induced drunk on your ass. And I didn't molest you, even though I have you on video begging me to join you in bed. I did what any good citizen would do—helped you to the bathroom to throw up, then let you sleep it off in my bed…by yourself."

"You probably drugged me. Maybe I'll go to an emergency room and have them test my blood." I'm bluffing because I have a vague memory of someone—not her—offering me some E, but I can't remember if I took it or not.

"If there are drugs in your system, they didn't come from me. Besides, you were at a party. There were drugs all over the place, so you could have gotten them from anybody."

I stare at her while my brain gropes for what's missing in this scenario. "Who are you? How did you get invited to Lisa's party?"

Her mocking smile fades for the first time, and she averts her gaze. "I came up from the beach."

Aha. "There's a six-foot stone wall and a locked gate between her property and the beach." Realization dawns. "You were trespassing. You're no better than scum-of-the-earth paparazzi."

"I am not paparazzi. I am an influencer and celebrity blogger. It's none of your business how I got into that party." She rushes forward, pushes me toward the door, and opens it. "You need to leave. Now."

She's nearly my height, but I'm a lot stronger, so I put a hand on the door frame to stop my forced march outdoors. My brain finally kicks into gear. This battle is not over. I lean forward so my face is inches from hers. "I'll call Lisa. She's a star and can get a judge to file an injunction against the release of your videos, then press charges against you for trespassing. Your nosy little ass will be cooling in a jail cell before this day is done."

Her smug expression returns. "Oh, yeah? It'll be a little hard to make a trespassing charge stick when I show police the video of you backing down Langston's bouncer by declaring that I was at the party as your guest." She visibly shudders. "I almost dropped my phone when you grabbed me and stuck your tongue in my mouth. Yuck." She shoves me hard, and I stumble backward into a breezeway that leads to the parking lot of her apartment complex. "Now get the hell out of my apartment."

"My car is still at Lisa's house."

She points to my phone, which is in my hand. "Call an Uber from the sidewalk." She slams the door in my face, and I hear the lock engage.

"Well, shit." I need to get home and call my agent so we can spin this as a joke. I can say I had been drinking and thought it would be funny to pretend the imagined lesbian relationship between Lisa's character and mine was real. That's it. I'll paint the whole thing as a prank.

CHAPTER TWO

They can't kill me." I stare at my agent. This is not happening. I'm a major secondary character in a top-rated show. They can't kill my character. They can't do this to me. THEY CAN'T DO THIS TO ME.

"They absolutely can," says Kylie, my agent and longtime friend. "And they have."

The past three weeks have been a downward spiral of events. Lisa Langston was outed, but her public-relations team had spun the video of her kissing Charleigh Long as a party game that was a playful acting challenge. The video of my rant about Lisa dumping me was presented as a sad mental breakdown of a young actor who harbored a secret crush on Lisa—a crush dangerously encouraged by fans' perception of real chemistry between the two actors. The video fiasco shut down production for two full weeks while the show's scripts were rewritten to kill off my character and introduce a male love interest for Lisa's character.

"How? How can they kill my character between episodes? The last one that aired has us at the cabin together. Does a bear eat me? The fans will never believe that." I still can't wrap my brain around this latest development. "How can they explain my character's death if I'm not on the show to set it up?" Wait. Maybe I just disappear, leaving room for me to come back from my supposed death after having amnesia or something.

"Lisa goes into town for breakfast groceries while you're still sleeping, and the cabin catches on fire and burns to the ground. Your corpse is an unrecognizable crispy critter, but they identify you by dental records and the hardware that doctors placed in your left leg after your skiing accident in season two."

"Anybody could have pins in their leg, and I don't have a single filling to identify me through dental records."

"Your character does."

I stand and pace. "I can't believe this."

"Did you think they could keep you on the show? Even after the damage control by Lisa's team, there was still the video of you naked and trying to seduce that woman. Our lawyers managed to get the social media idiots to ban it from their platforms, though practically every lesbian in the world had probably already downloaded and saved it to fuel their masturbation fantasies."

I cover my face and scream into my hands. I'll wait until an appropriate amount of time has passed so people won't think it's me, and then I'll wreck that blogger bitch's life. I'll slash her tires, pay some prostitute to seduce her boyfriend, break into her apartment and put some roadkill animal under her bed until it smells up her whole apartment. Roaches. Yeah. What was that movie where a neighbor was trying to get a couple to move out? I'll get a big jar of roaches and release them in her apartment. Except I'm not sure where to get a big jar of roaches. Crickets, then. You can buy those at bait shops, right? They aren't as gross but will drive her crazy with their chirping.

"Uh, I have more news." Kylie interrupts my plotting when she stands and comes around her desk to deliver her last blow.

I stop pacing and heave a long sigh that slumps my shoulders as I stare down at the floor. *How much did the Persian rug under my feet cost her?* "Good or bad?"

She clears her throat. "More like bad and worse."

"I need some good news."

She pauses. "You can go home for your mother's back surgery because you're no longer filming."

I love my mother, but I am not the sweet-caregiver type. Kylie knows this. "I've already hired round-the-clock nursing care for her."

"You might want to cancel that."

"Why?"

"You will not be paid for the past two weeks when you guys have not been filming."

I shrug. That's a blow, considering I'm currently out of work, but nothing I can't survive.

"Even worse, the studio's insurance company is suing you for the money lost while production was stalled."

Great. Out of work and broke.

❖

I slide my custom snow skis next to my scuba tanks and camping equipment piled in the rented storage space where I keep my toys, again thanking the lesbian gene that had persuaded me to buy a roomy Jeep instead of a sports car when the show became a hit and I was making good money. I'd thought my ramen days were behind me, but the settlement with the studio has left me with little more than fifteen hundred dollars in my bank account.

Like a lot of twenty-somethings, I rent a modest apartment, have bought minimal furniture, and spend the rest of my earnings on expensive toys and vacations. I'd deluded myself that I'd start investing some of my income next season. Only there wasn't going to be a next season. Not on *Judge and Jury* anyway. I slam the tailgate closed, square my shoulders, and tell myself that I'll be back by New Year's.

Sure, my name is dirt on the West Coast right now, but I'm taking Kylie's advice to lay low for a while. She didn't say how long but quietly informed me that she would be shown the door if she dared even whisper my name to a casting director.

My crime apparently isn't being a lesbian, but outing a major celebrity and getting drunk enough to be videoed while I ranted about her bed-hopping. I might have also dropped a few names of her past conquests. I still have no memory of the rant, but I threw up for thirty minutes after viewing the video online. My big mouth not only cost me my job, but it got me banned from every high-end lesbian bar within five hundred miles. The bouncers said they would lose customers because their businesses would no longer be viewed as a safe place for those who preferred to keep their gayness discreet.

So, I've sublet my apartment. I considered taking all my toys with me so I wouldn't have to keep paying for the storage space, but I didn't want to trailer my Jet Ski all the way across the country. Kylie said she'd try to get me some work on the East Coast. She had emphasized "try," but I had faith that my handsome face—a gift from my father—and my charming smile—inherited from my mother—would win me a role on some show filming on the East Coast so I could keep up the rent on the storage space. In the meantime, I'm hoping fifteen hundred dollars will buy enough gas, pizza, and burgers—because I can eat only so much ramen and mac-and-cheese—to get me from California to Pennsylvania.

❖

Another group of chatty teens just blew into the pizza parlor, and I slouch lower in my chair by the door, wrapping my arms around myself to ward off the unseasonably cold wind that follows them. Damn. I need to find the box I packed with my sweatshirts and jackets. *You're not in sunny California anymore, Dorothy.* Climate change sure has the weather screwed up. A cold front from Canada has dropped nighttime temperatures into the low forties, but they're expected to return to the mid sixties next week. After five years in sunny California, I'm freezing.

I'm mentally searching my packed Jeep when a large shadow falls over me, and I look up. The woman holding my pizza-to-go is built like a linebacker and sports a buzz cut that screams lesbian.

"That my pizza?" I ask.

"Stuffed crust with beef, mushrooms, green peppers?"

I normally order thin-crust, but I want this pizza to last several meals. "That's me. Thanks." I reach for the box of deliciousness, but she doesn't hand it over.

"You're Davis Hart, aren't you?"

I hesitate. Her tone is neutral, but I'm wary. It's been days since I've had a conversation with a human that wasn't at a drive-through speaker, and nearly a month since I've heard or read a kind word from any person other than Kylie. "Maybe you should give me my pizza before I answer that question."

She breaks into a grin and holds out the pizza box for me to take. It's warm in my hands and smells heavenly. "I knew it. Who would ever think Davis Hart would walk into my pizza joint?"

I relax with relief and return her smile. "I'm on my way to my hometown in Pennsylvania. My mom's having back surgery." That sounds better than admitting I'm fleeing my disaster of a career.

She waves to someone behind the counter, and a girl comes out with another pizza box and a white paper bag.

"It's her, really her?" the girl asks.

I chuckle. This is so good for my battered ego. "It's really me." I shoot her my trademark smile and wink. Okay. Winking is corny, but the girl nearly melts right in front of me.

The woman takes the bag and extra pizza box from the girl and stacks it on top of the box I'm holding. "Here's a dessert pizza, and the bag is full of cheesy bread and my special cinnamon bread. It's on the house."

"Wow. Thanks so much." I almost tear up at her kindness. "I don't want to get you into trouble with your boss, though."

"Not possible," she said, holding out her hand to shake mine. "I'm Rae Donovan, and this is my restaurant."

"It's nice to meet you, Rae. This is great. It should last me all the way to Pennsylvania. I won't have to stop again except to get gas and pee." I balance my bounty on one hand and motion for them to stand next to me. "How about a selfie with me? You have my permission to post it online, too, if you want."

Rae pulls her phone from her back pocket and snaps a few photos of the three of us, then a couple of just her and me. When we're done, she shakes my hand again. "I just want to say that you got a raw deal when they cut you from *Judge and Jury.* Those Hollywood bitches ought to be more careful of stomping on people's feelings if they don't want their dirty laundry hanging out for everyone to see."

I stare at my feet for a moment, searching for a reply. When I finally look up, I don't see a big-bodied woman sporting a buzz-cut and wearing a T-shirt stained with flour and pizza sauce. I gaze into crystal-blue eyes filled with compassion. "I appreciate that, but that's the way showbiz goes. It's a rough business. I'll be back after taking care of my mom for a few months." I just have to keep telling myself a new opportunity is right around the corner, and it will happen.

My heart is singing and my confidence renewed as I drive out of the Pizza-Pizza parking lot. Yep. The East Coast fans are a lot more forgiving. This relocation is definitely going to be my ladder back to the top.

CHAPTER THREE

D avis! Why didn't you tell me you were coming?"
I lean into my mother's hug, staggered by how good it feels. "I wanted to surprise you."

"I thought you were filming this month." She releases me and herds me into the kitchen, the center of our home where she has baked countless cookies for me and my friends, hosted family potlucks, and decorated her award-winning cakes.

I've been arguing with myself about what to tell her, but as I look into her brown eyes that are shining with the excitement of her only daughter's return, I know I have to confess the truth. Well, maybe not all of it. She doesn't have a problem with me being a lesbian, but she would have a problem with me sleeping with a married woman...even if Lisa's marriage is all for show because her husband is also gay. "The writers have killed my character in the upcoming episodes."

Her eyes go wide and her jaw drops. "They killed you?"

I nod and give her a crooked smile. "Yep. They needed a shocker to pump up the script. What better way to do that than kill off a major character?"

"You must have other offers." She goes to the refrigerator and pulls out the makings of a sandwich, without asking if I'm hungry. Food has always been her bandage for any of life's catastrophes. "That's why actors leave a good job, right? Because they have a better or more interesting offer?" She pauses, her stressed expression turning to wonder. "You've got an offer to film a movie. Oh, my goodness. Wait until the ladies at bingo night hear this!"

I wave away her assumption. "No, Mom. No movie. They're killing a character to boost ratings. Unfortunately, it's my character. That's showbiz. It happens. I haven't decided what offer to take next." Except that I'll take any offer to do anything right now. I can only live off my credit cards for so long before they'll expect payments. "Kylie is checking for something I can do on the East Coast for now. You know, so I can be closer to home while you're recovering from your surgery."

Mom slides the ham sandwich she's made over to me. "Oh, honey. You shouldn't worry about that. My friends already have set up a schedule for bringing me meals and sitting with me. I've called and canceled those nurses you hired. My insurance pays for a home healthcare nurse to check on me every day and change my bandage."

"I already knew that. The agency told me when I called to cancel the night nurse because I'll be here."

She came around the kitchen island to hug me again. "You're such a good daughter. I don't know what I did to deserve you."

I shrug and bite into my sandwich. "Just lucky, I guess." Yeah, yeah. If I hadn't gotten killed off the show, I would totally be the bad daughter hiring strangers to care for Mom while I worked and partied. Her friends would take care of her. I mean, what could I do from the West Coast? And I'm here now. Right?

❖

I pretend not to hear the whispers behind me while I stand in line at the local Starbucks.

"Is that Davis Hart?"

"Her mother lives here, you know. Maybe she's visiting."

"Do you think she'd mind if I asked for a selfie with her? I read that some celebrities are really rude if you bother them."

"My sister went to high school with her. She said she was an out lesbian and a real player even then."

"Damn. She's hotter in person than she is on TV."

I take my cue and turn around. "Hi, ladies. Can I help you with something?"

One of the foursome actually squeals.

"You're Davis Hart, aren't you?"

I smile. "That's what my mother named me."

The girl who dubbed me a player raised an eyebrow. "That's not a stage name?"

"Nope. I was named Davis after Bette Davis, my mother's favorite actress. And Hart is my real last name. If you don't believe me, ask anyone who had my mom as their third-grade teacher at Stallings Elementary."

"Could you order, please? You're holding up the line." The request comes from a stunning woman behind my group of admirers. Her hazel eyes stand out against her latte skin and full mane of brown curls.

"S-sorry." I whirl around to face the barista and hurriedly spit out my order. "Grande triple-shot Americana with room for cream. Name is Davis."

"Oh my God. You're Davis Hart," the barista says.

"Yes, sorry, but I don't want to hold up the line." I quickly repeat my order for her while I grab a napkin, glance at her name tag, and scribble *Heather, thanks for the great coffee. Davis Hart.*

She types in my order, writes my name on a cup, and smiles when I hand her the napkin. "Wow. Thanks."

"You're welcome." I step out of the line and head over to the counter where you wait for your order. The hazel-eyed goddess rolls her eyes at my groupies, who wait until they arrive at the register to debate their coffee orders. When they finally finish, she gives hers in clipped, precise words.

"Grande, triple-shot, medium roast."

"Room for cream?"

"No."

I love a woman who knows what she wants and isn't afraid to say it. So, naturally, I sidle over to where she is now waiting for her order after I pick up mine.

She instantly holds up a hand in a back-off gesture. "Don't waste your time. I'm too busy to watch TV, so I'm not familiar or impressed with your apparent celebrity status. Go back to your groupies."

"Ouch. I was hoping to impress you with my winning smile and adorable dimples." I point to my cheek.

"Asia," the barista calls out as he places a grande coffee on the counter.

My mystery woman reaches for the cup, then turns back to me. "I'm sorry. I don't mean to be rude, but I'm really busy and don't have time to swoon over you." With those parting words, she strides toward the door.

Damn, she's sexy. I have to find out more about her. How many women named Asia can live in a small town named Christmas?

That's right. It's Christmas year-round in my little hometown. We're a town of gift shops carrying unique—many locally crafted—items, holiday decorations, and real sleigh rides when the snow cooperates. I spent a lot of my teen years dressed as an elf for a series of part-time jobs. The foam ear points were kind of cool, but the costume was hella sweaty in July. Our little town of Christmas, of course, uses much more than its share of the power grid every summer as the stores crank up their air conditioning to simulate winter conditions, and Christmas lights twinkle through spring, summer, and fall.

I look for her when I step outside the coffee shop, but she's vanished like the hope Santa would finally bring me a pony one Christmas. So, I double back and interrupt the barista at the cash register.

"Hey. Do you know the woman with the amazing eyes who

was just in here?" Met with a blank stare, I elaborate. "Brown curly hair down to her shoulders, mocha skin, and light-colored eyes?" The stare is still blank. "Asia."

The girl blinks. "Oh. Yeah. Asia isn't a common name. No. I don't know her."

Damn. "Is she a regular customer? Or do you think she's a tourist?"

She shrugs as she punches in her current customer's order.

"I don't think she's a tourist, but she's new around here. She's been coming in about three times a week for the past month, I guess."

I perform a quiet fist-pump. "Thank you." I stuff a fiver in her tip jar and practically jog back out to the street. Just in case Asia might have reappeared, I look both ways down Main Street. My new infatuation is nowhere in sight. No matter. I have her name, and I can stake out the coffee shop if necessary to initiate a second, hopefully more productive, totally accidental meeting. She'll go home or to work and google me, then kick herself for not welcoming my advances. Hell, all I'll need to do is put myself in her line of sight and graciously accept her apologies. Yep. The old Davis Hart charm will work its magic, and she'll be mine.

❖

"Oh my God. Davis. You're here!"

I throw up my arms in a classic Megan Rapinoe victory sign at Tommy Goldstein's excited greeting and strut down the aisle of the old theater where a group of community actors perform rotating holiday-themed plays year-round.

"'I'll be home for Christmas,'" he warbles.

Tommy was one of my besties throughout high school and college. After college, I left to seek my fortune on the West Coast, and Tommy came home to Bruce, the love of his life, and to teach drama to high-schoolers.

"Stop, stop." I wave my arms around like I'm clearing the air of his song. "It's not even Thanksgiving yet, and I don't know if I'll still be here for Christmas. I might be working somewhere."

I gather his tall body in a long hug. "I missed you, man."

He steps back, wiping his eyes. "I missed you, too." He's always been emotional. His strawberry-blond hair, freckles, slight physique, and flamboyant tendency often made him the target of bullies until we became best friends. I was athletic and popular despite being openly gay. Anyone who messed with him had to answer to me.

Others begin to emerge from backstage, whispering to each other about this visit from a real celebrity. I wave at them. My ego is still healing after the Lisa fiasco, so I need to absorb all their adoration for Davis Hart right now.

Then a slow clap sounds as Susan Schwartz emerges from the shadows of the stage. "Years later, she returns to the scene of her crime."

Crap. The girlfriend I left behind without saying good-bye. I drop my chin and draw on my best acting skills to look as repentant as possible. "I am so sorry, Susan, for not finding you before I left. But can you really blame a girl from a small town with stars in her eyes? That's not an excuse, but give me a chance to explain, uh, apologize over coffee…maybe sometime this week?"

She squints for a long minute as if thinking hard about how to respond. The silence in the empty theater is so loud, I almost jump when she finally speaks. "Hmm. Let me see. Not if you were the only other person left on this earth. We were together for two years. You said you loved me and wanted to have children with me."

"Ouch. I guess I deserve that," I said, hoping to drop the curtain on this scene. In my defense, I said that when I was naked and in a postcoital bliss. I've never even thought about sharing a pet with someone, much less having children. When I got the call to audition for *Judge and Jury*, I barely said good-bye to my mother. I was hired the same day I met with the show's casting director and didn't even come back for my clothes. The check the studio put in my hands when I signed a contract was plenty to rent an apartment and buy a more LA style wardrobe. "I can see you're still angry."

Her smile was more of a snarl. "Doesn't matter. Karma's a bitch, and from what I've read in the entertainment rags, that bitch got you dropped from your show. Now you've come home with your tail between your legs."

I disappoint her again if she's hoping to get a reaction from me. I've spent my years in LA watching some of the best actors work and honing my own skills in improv classes. Working this scene, I hop onto the stage and swagger over to her. "That's where you're wrong, babe. That whole situation was staged to get the most publicity out of my leaving the show for some opportunities here on the East Coast. My agent is fielding some theater projects for me right now." The lie comes as easily as reading a line of script.

A handsome, soft-butch woman I haven't noticed before tugs on Susan's sleeve. "Let it go, Susie. She's not worth getting upset." She gives me a disdainful look. "Real feelings go only as deep as their tans in Hollywood."

Susan seems to melt into the woman's side, sliding an arm around her waist as the woman drapes an arm over Susan's shoulders. "You're right, babe. She was a lousy fuck anyway." She gives me one last withering glare and turns away.

Nobody speaks as the two exit and the backstage door closes behind them. Finally, Tommy breaks the silence with a dramatic hand to his cheek.

"Ex-girlfriends. Whew."

I paste on a smile and turn to him. "You got that right." I slap my hands together, the sound echoing in the cavernous theater like a clapperboard used to mark the beginning of a new scene. I glance at the door where Susan exited. "So, who's the white knight defending Susan's honor?"

"That's Andie McCann. They met on a lesbian cruise about a year after you left, and Andie moved here a year after that. She owns a handywoman business that's pretty popular around town and builds sets for our productions." He heaves a huge sigh and sweeps his arm outward to indicate the empty auditorium. "Of course, there's not much to produce these days."

"What? You aren't currently doing a play?" Then it dawns on me that it's Saturday and a matinee should be underway. The others who had appeared to see the celebrity now disappear into the backstage darkness or gather in small groups for conversations that don't include me and Tommy.

"We never managed to really come back after the pandemic shut everything down for a year. We always operated on the money from the previous year's ticket sales, so we didn't have anything in the bank to put on a show when things reopened."

"What about some of that federal payroll money that was handed out to businesses?"

He gives a disgusted snort. "Yeah, well. All that money went to businesses owned by the politicians' friends. Or state legislatures just kept it to use for other stuff after the pandemic was over."

"Bastards." I've always hated politicians. "They only serve the rich people who fund their election campaigns."

"Yeah, well, one of those old rich men had a nostalgic moment and got us started up again. But he insists we stick to the same play all year to cut costs, and he made us cast his nephew as the lead. We lost most of our best actors because the nephew couldn't act worth crap but tried to tell everybody else what to do. Susan's planning to leave, too. Half the staff quit. Brent works at Home Depot over in Websonville, and Sadie went back to her mother's dress shop."

So, they'd lost their stage manager and wardrobe mistress. "Sadie swore she'd never go back there because her mother's clients were all on Medicare and dress like it's still the seventies," I say.

"Well, a girl has to pay the rent, you know. She's trying to be positive about it. She says she's getting experience in period fashion."

Sadie always was a glass-half-full person. Their absence, however, didn't explain why the theater was empty on a Saturday afternoon in October.

We sit down on the stage, dangling our legs over the edge as we face the bleakly empty seats. "If this guy is backing the play, why isn't a matinee happening right now?"

"Nobody wants to see the same old play again and again. After that first year back, we couldn't even fill the main floor, much less the mezzanine and boxes. So, we're only running a show from Thanksgiving through New Year's Day this year."

"You're kidding."

"No. I'm not. It's hurt the whole town. People came here just to see the plays we put on, then spent money in the gift shops. A lot of them are dependent on their online sales now, since the tourist numbers are down."

We both contemplate this absence of tourists while several more people arrive and join the low voices backstage. Something doesn't fit. They're here to practice nearly two months before they open a play they've performed hundreds of times?

"You're already getting ready for your December opening? Don't you guys have that play down by now?"

He shrugs. "We don't know why we're here. We all got an email from someone named Asia du Muir to be here today at four o'clock for a meeting about the upcoming production. It sounds like a made-up name, doesn't it? We have no idea who she is— maybe the niece of our benefactor who has suddenly decided theater might be fun, or a drag queen the old man is secretly plowing?"

I barely hear his peevish rant. Her name is Asia. Is du Muir of French origin? It has to be. Her beautiful face and obvious mixed-race heritage are so romantic, and I'm so smitten, it has to be French. It also would explain the soft lilt of her slight accent. I begin to imagine an entire backstory for her...immigrating to the United States after her parents divorce or are tragically killed in an accident, or maybe coming to the US to attend an Ivy League college. Maybe she's a Dreamer, brought here by her mother as a child.

"No. You're wrong," I say. I'm very aware of my breathy, almost whispering, tone. The thought of meeting her again is sucking the very breath from my lungs. Okay. I can be rather dramatic too, but, hey, I am an actor. It's in my DNA.

Tommy turns to stare at me. "You know her?"

I give myself a mental shake and slide into my go-to cocky persona. "No, but I want to. The woman I saw in the coffee shop this morning is a queen."

"You are such a dog. How do you know it's that same woman?"

"I heard the barista call out her name when her coffee was ready. How many women named Asia do you think are in this town?"

"Good point, but inconclusive."

We both look to the back of the auditorium when we hear the entrance door close, then the clomp of heeled boots sounds in the building's lobby. "I guess we're about to find out," I say.

Tommy turns to call over his shoulder. "Hey, everybody. I think she's here."

Except for Tommy and Susan, who has returned, the faces that gather at our backs are new to me. I've been gone for five years, but I wasn't expecting a nearly complete turnover of cast and crew. Several of the players I cut my acting teeth among had been with this community theater for twenty-plus years. It spoke to the slow death of this once-thriving group, but I'd mull that thought over later. Right now, I'm watching my queen emerge from the dimly lit upper seats into the bright lights of the stage's apron. Damn, she's gorgeous.

She stares at me. "I wasn't aware you were part of this group."

I try to look nonchalant. "I just dropped by to visit some old friends. This is where I got my start."

Her look is dismissive. "Well, you might want to take off. We're about to begin our first meeting."

"Don't mind me. I'll just sit quietly and listen. Tommy and I are going out for a drink when he's done here."

"We are?" he asks.

"Yes. We are. I'm buying," I say.

"I'd rather you wait in your car or in the lobby. I'd prefer whatever we talk about to remain among this group, not show up in gossip rags."

Ha. She does know who I am. I shake my head but smile at her. "I don't like those rags either. So we're on the same page."

She contemplates this remark for a quick second, then shrugs and turns her attention to the group. "Hello, everyone. I'm Asia du Muir. We'll be producing a new play, written by me and underwritten by a grant that is funding my post-doctorate fellowship at Columbia University."

"So, Mr. Fogel isn't backing the Christmas play?" Several of the new kids reveal their feelings about this by grinning prematurely.

"No. He is not." Asia pauses as if she wants to say more but stifles the impulse. "The grant will pay for costumes, set materials, utilities, and limited salaries for some staff and actors who win major roles in the play."

A titter of excitement is checked by cautious rumbling among the group. "So, we're having auditions?" someone asks.

Asia seems puzzled. "Of course."

One slender, dark-haired boy speaks up. "It's just that for the past couple of years, Mr. Fogel dictated who would get what role, without holding auditions. He always put his nephew, who was awful, in a leading role." Most of the group nod in agreement.

Asia shakes her head. "My fellowship is mentored by an off-Broadway producer and director. He'll expect this show to be run like a professional production."

"Who?" I'm so surprised, I forget to stay quiet. "Who's mentoring your fellowship?"

She frowns at me. "You are interrupting our meeting. Please leave."

I thrust my chin out in defiance. "I might want to audition."

Someone squeals, and the group emits a chorus of "yes" and "awesome."

"No." She pins me with an emotionless stare as the chatter dies out. "Let me be plain this time. Get out."

"Seriously?"

"Seriously. You are interrupting our meeting and distracting the group." Her gaze doesn't waver.

Did I seriously call her my queen? More like queen bitch. I don't need her condescension. At that moment, my phone buzzes in my pocket. I pull it out, read the identified caller, and stand. "My agent. I have to take this." I stride out with my phone to my ear as if I'm leaving because of the phone call, not because she ordered me out.

"Hey, Kylie. What'cha got for me?"

"Do you know how to cook?"

"What? You called me to swap recipes?"

"No, idiot. I want to get you on the *Wok-ee Wu* show as a guest cook."

"This is a joke, right?"

Her sigh is audible. "Look, Davis. I'm trying my best. Nobody wants to touch you yet. You can either give it some time or take whatever I can beg for you. This show has great ratings on the Food Network, and it's shot in Atlanta."

"Kylie, really. I don't know about this. I do good to heat up stuff in the microwave."

"How did you survive in college?"

"I was on the meal plan at the student cafeteria during the week and ate takeout on weekends."

"Okay. What's your favorite food cooked in a wok?"

"What's a wok?"

She sighs again. "You're hopeless. Go home and ask your mom for help. You don't have to know how to cook anything. Just get her to teach you the basics so you don't look completely stupid on the show."

A cooking show, of all things. "Okay. I'll do it, but only because my bank account is empty and I'm living off my credit cards."

"Did I mention they'll pay all your expenses? I'll text you the details and your plane ticket later this week."

"Okay." I pause. "Hey, Kylie?"

"Yeah?"

"I'm thinking I'd like to get back to my roots and do some theater, so look for some opportunities there, okay? I'll even take an off-Broadway role."

"Really?"

"Yeah. If I have to lay low, I want to have a little fun."

❖

"No! You're going to be on *Wok-ee Wu?*" Tommy did a little happy dance in his chair. "That's my favorite show. Bruce works second shift at the sheriff's office, so I record it each week for us to watch together on his day off." He leans over the table between us and whispers as if someone could be listening. "Sometimes I watch while it records, but I don't tell him. He thinks I wait for him."

I'm only half listening to him because Queen Asia has entered the coffee shop and is standing in line to give her order. "So, Tommy. What else did you guys talk about at your meeting yesterday?"

He grimaces. "Nothing secret, but a few surprises."

My eyes are still glued to her, but my ears are all his. "Surprises?"

"Yeah. You heard she's holding auditions."

"That makes sense. You've got a lot of newbies in the group."

He nods. "Yeah, but she's made deals with Columbia and NYU to let any of their theater students who audition and win roles get a grade in their current drama classes and finish their other semester classes online. The competition is going to be tough."

I nod, because he's right. "You'll be fine."

"No, I won't." I see real panic in his eyes. "She's doing cold reads. I won't even see the lines until the audition, so there's no practicing for it."

Asia picks up her order, then glances over at our table before heading our way. He has his back to her, unaware she's even in the shop.

"Chill, man. She's here and coming over to us."

"Shit." He goes rigid all over.

"Just act casual." I slump back in my seat and smile as she approaches. "Hi. How's the play going?"

She actually smiles back and stops by our table. "Great, so far. Auditions start Saturday, but the weekend spots are booked for the out-of-towners. I figure it'll be easier for local people to audition during the week." She turns to Tommy. "I know you'll want to audition next week, but I was hoping you'd be free to help run the weekend auditions."

"Me?" Tommy looks my way, his expression a mixture of surprise and uncertainty.

I raise my eyebrows and give him an encouraging nod.

"Uh, yeah. Sure. What time should I be there?"

"I didn't want to start too early because it's more than an hour for those students driving from the city. So, about eight thirty. The first audition is at nine. We'll break for lunch at one, then resume from two until seven. Then we'll do the same on Sunday."

Now I'm surprised. "You have that many college students who want to audition?"

She shrugs. "Yes, but I expect most are more interested in getting an instant grade in their drama class than acting in my play. Despite what students in other majors think, senior drama classes are tough."

I shake my head at my personal memory of college. "Professor Braddock's class was."

Asia raises both elegant eyebrows in a surprised expression. "You went to Columbia?"

"Yes. I did, but I didn't graduate because I got the call to audition for *Judge and Jury* in LA and never came back to finish." I don't add that I was flunking everything except my drama classes and quit before graduating because Professor Braddock was aware of my academic failings and leaned on an old friend to get me the audition.

Tommy jumps back into the conversation. "Davis is going to be taping the *Wok-ee Wu* show in two weeks."

Asia frowns, her brows drawing together.

"You know, on the Food Channel," he says to prompt her.

"Oh, right."

But I can see that, like me, she's never watched the show, and she begins to back away.

Tommy catches on, too, and changes the subject. "What will you need me to do Saturday?"

She stops. "I want to video each audition so I can review them all later. So we need to set marks on the stage and position the cameras. We'll be filming with deactivated phones. I have two with tripods, but it would be better with three."

Tommy practically wiggles with excitement. "I have an old iPhone and a tripod for it, too."

"Good. We can use both. We can connect them to the theater's Wi-Fi," Asia says.

"You use the cameras on old phones?" I'm amazed.

"Yes. You can't talk on them, but they still function as cameras," Tommy says. "I can even network them, then edit together auditions you're interested in reviewing."

Asia's mouth falls open, and she surges forward to grasp Tommy's shoulder. "That would be so helpful. Thank you." She dials her excitement back as if she suddenly realizes her aloof cool has been blown. "But do you have time to do that?"

Tommy waves away her concerns. "Honey, I have all the time in the world. I teach high school, but my husband works second shift, so I have my evenings free."

"Fantastic. See you on Saturday, then." She again backs away but waves at Tommy before turning to leave. It's like I'm not even here.

"I could help, too."

Tommy is in full queen mode now, waving his index finger in a no-you-won't gesture. "You would be a distraction," he says, echoing Asia's declaration from the previous day.

CHAPTER FOUR

"Hello?"

"Hey. Is this Janie? This is your Aunt Davis. Is your dad home?"

"I'm not supposed to talk to strangers." My cute little toddler niece has grown into an eight-year-old smart-ass while I was gone.

"I'm not a stranger. I'm your aunt." My explanation is met with silence. "I'm your dad's sister."

"Is this a scam? Because I don't think my father has a sister."

Okay. Maybe I haven't been home for five years, but I know they must have gossiped about me at their holiday gatherings. This kid is just being a punk. I'll get her back later.

"Just tell your dad the phone's for him."

"What's the magic word?"

I grind my teeth. "Please put your dad on the phone."

Thunk. She drops Bryan's phone and screams, "Dad. Phone."

"Yeah?"

"Hey, it's me, Davis."

"I'm sorry. Davis who?"

"Very funny, bro."

"Ah, the prodigal daughter. Let me guess. You've been kicked out of the Hollywood pigsty and have come home to beg Mom to forgive you for all the birthdays and holidays when you forgot to even call?"

"Don't judge what you know nothing about, okay? I'm deciding between new possibilities now, and I've asked Kylie to consider offers on the East Coast so I can be closer to home and see family more. I also asked her to hold off until after Mom's surgery, so I can help take care of her."

After a few seconds of silence, he drops his sarcasm when he speaks. "Davis, you've never even taken care of a pet."

I frown. "I took care of my hamster, Buster."

"For about a week. Then Mom moved him to my room so I'd tend to him. I wanted a rat, not a hamster, because they're a million times smarter."

I don't care how old we are. We'll always revert to six-year-old siblings. "I gave you my hamster so you'd quit whining. Mom was never going to let a rat in her house."

"That's the Davis I remember. Nothing is ever the golden girl's fault because she can do no wrong. But I know you didn't call just to bicker with me about a long-dead hamster. What's up?"

I'm reluctant to ask the favor and give him one more chance to shoot me down. He already has enough arrows in that quiver, but he'll find out if I ask one of Mom's friends instead. "Like I said, I asked Kylie to hold off on any jobs until Mom's surgery, but she's signed me up to be a guest on some Food Channel show, and they're taping on the day of Mom's surgery. Can you possibly be at the hospital with her instead?"

He gives a derisive snort. "I'd planned to be there anyway, so whether you can make it or not doesn't really matter."

Damn. When did he grow so bitter? "I'm flying back right after we finish taping. I'll be at the hospital as soon as I'm wheels down and can drive in from JFK."

He seems to relent. "Okay. I'll text you when we hear she's out of surgery and let you know what room she'll be in."

"Thanks, Bryan. I need to do this show to start establishing myself on the East Coast, or I would have turned it down." A small lie, but I hadn't realized he was so mad at me and want to make things good with him.

"Sure. Talk to you soon."

❖

"This is awesome, man. I didn't realize you knew how to do this." I was bored to tears sitting around the house, and Tommy was happy to show off his editing skills. The auditions were better than expected, but then he told me Asia had already deleted the ones she said had no chance.

"Yeah. I post a lot on TikTok and make a bit of money on the side editing videos that people shoot at weddings, birthday parties, and other events."

"Have you thought about editing for film and television?" I'm impressed with his natural selection skills as I watch over his shoulder.

He shrugs. "Honestly, I don't think I'd like the pressure of those jobs. I love teaching high-schoolers and taking only the editing jobs I want."

"Dude, wedding videos?"

He stops his work and turns to face me. "I mean this in the kindest way, Davis, but I feel like the work I do really matters. Fifty years from now, it's doubtful anyone will be watching reruns of *Judge and Jury*. But that wedding video I edited last week will still be watched when that twenty-something couple is in their seventies, then maybe even generations later by their offspring. It's a real history of ordinary people, not actors performing fictional stories."

"But you're never going to make a lot of money doing that."

"Bruce and I are financially quite comfortable. I don't need to be wealthy. We're very rich in friends here. And I have students I taught five years ago who still keep in touch to let me know how they're doing."

Wow. When did Tommy grow up to be such an adult? I hunch my shoulders and pretend to be intent on the scene frozen on his screen. I have lots of friends out in LA, all of whom quit taking my calls post-Lisa. Time for a subject change. "I talked to my brother yesterday."

"How did that go?" He starts the audition video again, pausing occasionally to make an editing mark.

"Okay. I've got to be in Atlanta to tape that cooking show the day Mom has surgery. He's promised to call me when she's done and let me know her room number."

"That's good. Last time I ran into him, I asked how his sister was doing, and he said, 'What sister? Do I have a sister?'"

I'm flooded with shame, an unfamiliar emotion. "I didn't realize he resented me so much."

"He's done pretty good for himself, starting his own construction company. Bruce tried to hire him last year to renovate our master bath, but Bryan apologized and said his crews were all booked up through the end of the year. We had to go with somebody else."

"He's pissed that I didn't come home more, but I was working." Defensiveness supplants any shame I'm feeling. "My niece didn't even know who I was when she answered the phone, so I'm pretty sure he doesn't let her watch my show."

Tommy gives me a sidelong look. "Please. Janie brags to anyone who will listen about her aunt who's on television. She was just yanking your chain." He taps a few keys to wrap up the audition he's editing. We both settle in to watch the guy on the screen.

"He's pretty good," Tommy says.

I shake my head. "He's reading for television, not theater. His expressions are too understated and his movements too wooden."

The video cuts to a different scene where the guy has to sing. "She's written a musical?"

"Not really. She says there are a few songs, but all are public domain because she has more important things to spend the grant money on."

His singing is terrible. "You sing a lot better than that. If that's the part you want, your singing alone will land it."

We gaze at each other and break into a duet from our old theater days about the sun coming up tomorrow.

We stop after a few lines and laugh together, and then Tommy shakes his head. "Understudy, maybe." He closes that file and opens another one. "Look at this guy."

We watch a very handsome guy's audition tape. He's obviously had experience onstage, and his full, rich voice is mesmerizing.

"I see what you mean. He'll be hard to beat for that part, but there have to be other male characters you'd be great playing."

"She's also got a couple of women whose auditions are just as good," he says, ignoring my encouragement.

"Have you seen a full script yet?"

"No. She's either keeping it secret or doesn't want to admit that she hasn't finished it."

"I'd like to see it when you get a copy."

"How do you know I'll even make the cast?"

"Because you're good, Tommy. You could have made it if you'd come to LA with me. When you and Bruce have a spat, don't you ever look at him and think, 'I could be famous if I hadn't stayed here for you'?"

"Davis, Davis, Davis. Look into my eyes." He grabs my chin to direct my gaze at his face and waits while I avert my eyes in several different directions before complying. "I am happy with my life. I love my students, my coworkers, and, most of all, Bruce. Even extreme fame couldn't give me the love and happiness I have every day."

"Fame gets you adoring fans and a free pass to the front of the line waiting to be admitted to restaurants and nightclubs. It also gets you lots of money and all the beautiful men you can handle."

"Having my meal interrupted by an autograph-seeking fan every time I go out to eat, getting drunk at parties, and sleeping with people I don't know or care about. I've outgrown any dream I had for all that, Davis."

He doesn't deliver his revelation like a criticism, but it still cuts deep, and my defensive shields spring up. "Well, I still like to party, and I don't care if I don't know her name as long as the fuck is good." The sadness in his eyes stops me, and I grasp his forearm. "Hey, we just want different things. Maybe someday I'll feel like settling down, but I still love the carefree life." I lightly punch him on the arm. "If that changes, you'll be the first to know."

"Okay." He closes his laptop. "Want to go with me? I'm meeting Asia at the theater to go over the edited auditions."

I give him a nonchalant shrug as I drawl out my answer. "I guess I have time." Inside, I'm jumping up and down. Yes, yes, yes! I'm going to see her again.

❖

Asia gives Tommy a warm smile when he enters the sound-and-lighting booth. "Hey. I'm surprised you've finished editing the weekend's auditions already. We were just completing an equipment check." She ignores the fact that I'm trailing behind Tommy.

"All of this—the booth, lighting, and sound equipment—were installed new right before everything shut down for a year. So the system hasn't been used that much. It should operate like new," he says, placing his laptop on the booth's console. "Ready to have a look?"

"Yes." Asia rubs her hands together in clear anticipation.

I stay quiet for now, content to observe and find out what I can learn about her.

"What do you want to see first? Bad to good or vice versa?" Tommy asks.

"Hopefully, we ruled out the bad ones. So let's look at good to really good."

I like her optimism and can't contain myself any longer. "How many roles are you looking to fill?"

If her sidelong look were a bullet, I'd be mortally wounded. Still, she answers my question. "The story is about a couple—he's Catholic and she's Jewish—who aren't particularly religious. They've just moved back to the United States after serving in the Peace Corps, and their parents are astonished to discover the couple has a two-year-old. Now both grandparents are pressuring the couple to celebrate the holidays with them and to observe their religious traditions for the sake of the child. So, eight real speaking roles—the parents, the four grandparents, a rabbi, and a priest…nine if you count the maid that the young mother goes to for advice."

I sit back in the chair I've pulled up so I can peek over their shoulders. "Wow. That's an ambitious cast for community theater."

She stiffens and gestures for Tommy to open the first file. "I think we've pulled enough talent from the university programs to do it. Besides, we haven't even held local auditions yet. Some of you guys have been doing this type of thing successfully for years, so you must have some good actors among the locals."

"I'm glad to know you plan to give them a fair chance, and not just go with the university students." I know I haven't been around for a while, but I feel protective of the theater group I once considered my second family.

Tommy looks over his shoulder at me. "You said you'd be quiet and just watch."

I throw up my hands and mimic closing a zipper over my mouth.

He returns his attention to the laptop. "Okay. Here's the first one."

They spend almost two hours haggling over the videos.

"Except for the rabbi and priest, I think we have decent candidates for the major roles," Asia says, sounding pleased. "I'm sure about the two who will play the couple, but the grandparent roles aren't locked in. We might see somebody better among the locals." She checks a leatherbound notebook she seems to always have with her. "But last time I checked the board, only a handful had signed up."

Tommy closes his laptop. "Yeah. A lot of people quit the group when the year-round production slimmed down to only a few months a year. Others quit because of Mr. Fogel."

"Do you think you could persuade some of them to audition?" Asia looks to Tommy with hope in her eyes. "I really envisioned someone older than twenty-five playing either the priest or the rabbi."

"I can try," he says.

I almost throw up my hand and shout "Oh, oh, oh," like Horshack in that old television show *Welcome Back, Kotter*. The figurative zipper on my mouth flies open. "What about Ray? He'd be perfect in one of those roles. Is he still around?"

Tommy shakes his head. "I don't know. His wife died of COVID during the first months of the pandemic. After Mr. Floyd said there wasn't any role for him in his play, Ray just kind of disappeared. His neighbor, who's a friend of my mother, said he rarely ventures past his mailbox anymore."

"I'll go see him. He used to love Mom's chicken casserole. I'll get her to bake one for him."

Tommy frowns. "Aren't you flying to Atlanta tomorrow?"

"Not till late. I'll get Mom to make something for him tonight. Then you and I can take it to him at lunch tomorrow. Mom's surgery is the day after tomorrow."

"Can't. I'm scheduled to audition tomorrow."

I point to the empty stage. "Audition for Asia now."

Tommy's leg begins to bounce. I've caught him off guard, but I happen to know he works best when he's under pressure.

"We're not set up to film it, and nobody's here to read lines with me."

"I'll read with you. We've been on the stage together a hundred times. You know we can do it."

I expect Asia to jump in and stop me, but she looks curious.

Tommy's shaking his leg and his head now. "No. You just don't want to go see Ray by yourself."

"Fine. Mom will go with me to Ray's house tomorrow. But you need to read with me now."

"I'm sure Asia wants to head home," Tommy says.

She begins rummaging in her messenger bag. "No. This is fine." She holds up some papers. "I've got the pages you need to read right here."

I pause and issue the challenge neither of us has ever backed down from since grade school. "I dare you."

Tommy glares at me, then snatches the pages from Asia. "Fine. I'll do it."

Asia reaches for the lighting board and brings up the stage lights. "I'll come down there to watch since we aren't taping."

The three of us traipse down a long aisle, and then Tommy and I hop up onto the stage.

Asia digs in her messenger bag again and retrieves a thick stack of papers held together by a clip, then flips through the pages. "Let's do the scene where Rebecca is arguing with Rabbi Goldman...pages fifty through fifty-six. Davis, you read Rebecca, and Tommy can read the rabbi's lines."

I stifle the automatic "duh" on my lips at her instruction but, honestly, give Tommy a wig and he could totally pull off the Rebecca role. We shuffle through our sheets to locate the right pages, then take a few minutes to glance through them. When I'm ready, I put the pages in order and look at Tommy. "Let me know when you want to start."

He does a great job reading the lines of a progressive rabbi, who insists that religion lives in the heart, not in rituals. Asia seems pleased by his performance, but I pull him to the side and propose that he change his body language to that of a much older man and ad-lib his lines a little. This is something we did a lot as kids practicing for our roles.

"Okay if we try that again, a little differently this time?"

Asia seems surprised but hesitantly agrees.

Tommy's physical changes are subtle—a slight hunch to his shoulders and bend at his waist, a slackening of his jaw, and a tendency to tug at his earlobe. I give Rebecca's lines a bit more urgency and agitation, which lets Tommy expand his character as a calming presence.

Asia responds with a slow clap when we finish. "That was great, you guys." Her smile is the first she's ever directed my way and lights up the room. Okay, it was mostly for Tommy, but I'm claiming it as partly mine for helping him shine.

"Thank you," I say, giving her an exaggerated bow.

"Davis makes it easy," Tommy says. "We've worked a lot of roles together since elementary school."

She digs around in her messenger bag again, pulls out a few papers, then joins us on the stage. She hands the new pages to Tommy but keeps the full script in her hands. "I want you to read a scene with me. You're the rabbi and I'm Rebecca."

Tommy nails his part, but Asia does a few things I'd correct. I'm about to blurt them out when she asks Tommy if he'd change anything in the scene.

"Well…"

"Go ahead," she says. "Tell me what you'd do differently."

He points to the stage direction with one dialogue. "I'd have Rebecca face the audience when she turns her back to the rabbi, instead of turning backstage. You can't hear her lines with her facing that direction."

Asia smiles. "Good. What else?"

"I'd have the rabbi sit, while Rebecca uses up the stage, pacing as she talks. She's looking for a figurative anchor for her thoughts and feelings about her Jewish heritage. He should stay stationary. He can rotate his body in her direction as he reaches out to her with answers but should never get up from his stationary point."

"Excellent!" Asia and I shout this together, then look at each other, and her eyebrow rises. I mimic a zipper closing my mouth, but she continues talking to Tommy. "Why aren't you at least with an off-Broadway production? You're that good."

He shakes his head. "I'm happy here. I love my students and my husband. I wouldn't be happy traveling with a show."

Her smile is sad. "I envy you. Knowing what you want and going for it without apology is rare."

Tommy blushes, his red cheeks evident even under the stage lights. "Thanks. Most people don't understand. They think I'm stupid or scared and throwing away my potential."

She steps toward him and squeezes his arm. "I think you're very brave." She gathers the sheets of dialogue from us and hops off the stage to retrieve her bag. "Thanks for everything. Can you upload those auditions to the Google Drive and share them with me? I'm pretty sure which ones I like best, but I'd like to look at a couple of them again."

"Sure. I'll do that tonight. We had a half day at school today, but now it's back to a full schedule until the Thanksgiving break. I can still come in the evenings this week to help film the local auditions."

"I hate taking up so much of your time, but that would be awesome."

"It's no problem." He drops his gaze to his feet. "We're all grateful you're doing this. We realize this is probably our last production because people don't seem to want to crowd into a theater anymore, and we didn't want one of Mr. Fogel's productions to be our last."

"They might not be so grateful when they find out the stars of this community theater play won't be from this community." I almost slap my hand over my traitorous mouth and have started to backpedal when Asia's laser-glare cuts through me. "I mean, that's not a criticism...just an observation. You know, to get ready for. I'm sure they'll realize, though, you have a lot riding on this...your fellowship and all." I'm babbling, something I haven't done since my mom caught me and my eighth-grade crush experimenting with a little girl-on-girl in my bedroom.

Tommy's hand flies to his mouth, and his face features a no-you-didn't expression. I'm melting like Oz's Wicked Witch of the West when she finally speaks.

"I have more than you can fathom—maybe my whole career—riding on this project, and I don't need some Hollywood party girl messing with my staff." She shoulders her bag and marches up the aisle and out through the doors.

Tommy waits until we hear the outside one slam. His hand on his hip, he turns to me. "How does that foot in your mouth taste?"

I straighten. "I was just telling the truth. You got a pat on the head for being 'brave' when you spoke it. I get a cold shoulder."

He shakes his head. "Sometimes you are so clueless."

CHAPTER FIVE

F irst, I'll walk you quickly through the basics of stir-fry for our new audience, and then you will help me make a surprise dish." The chef is physically a stereotypical Asian, but he sounds as American as a cheeseburger and has a faint Southern accent.

"A surprise dish?"

"Yeah. When we're done, you get to sample it."

"Okay. Sounds easy." We're standing next to a waist-high butcher-block island with six jumbo shrimp, scallions, and green, yellow, and red bell peppers that have already been cored and seeded. We both are wearing *Wok-ee Wok* full aprons and chef hats like the guys who cook hibachi for customers in Japanese restaurants. This is going to be fun.

"Rolling cameras in five, four, three, two." The floor manager counts it off on his fingers until he gets to the silent "one," then points to indicate the cameras are rolling.

The chef bows slightly to the camera and suddenly assumes an Asian accent, clipping his words and leaving some out as if he isn't fluent in English. The change catches me by surprise, but I quickly school my expression and smile at the camera.

"Welcome to *Wok-ee Wok*." He pauses for the applause sign to turn off and the audience to quiet. "Thank you. Thank you. Two surprises for you today—our guest, Davis Hart, and my favorite Korean stir-fry. Both hot and spicy, yes?" He pauses again and wiggles his eyebrows suggestively as the audience obeys the applause sign.

"Thanks, Chef Wu. I'm tickled to be here because I love a good stir-fry." Not really, but this is acting, right? I do like hibachi, but I always ask them to skip the vegetables. So, stir-fry? Way too many veggies for me. I do like those crunchy little water chestnuts and always ask for them when I order fried rice.

"Good. You have wok at home for cooking?" He nods, and I find myself nodding with him.

"Yes. I do." I'm pretty sure that thing hanging on the wall in the kitchen is shaped like the one on the burner in front of us. Who knew you could cook in it? I thought it was just wall decoration. But I do cook. I can scramble eggs and spread butter and jam on toast. Oh, and cream cheese on a bagel I've toasted in the toaster.

"What do you stir-fry most?"

I think quickly and blurt out the first thing that comes to mind. "Shrimp fried rice." At least that's what I order a lot for takeout. And I do know how to clean and boil shrimp.

"Excellent. We have rice, shrimp, and scallions here. Let's start with preparing the shrimp." He hands me a knife and places a bowl of water between us before handing me a shrimp.

I pick up one, glad that they're jumbo. This will be easy. "Here's a cooking tip," I tell the audience. I'm getting into this now. "The shell of the shrimp contains a lot of flavor. So, if you're boiling them, rather than frying, you should just cut through the shell to devein them, but wait until they're boiled to remove the shell."

Proud to have contributed something to the task, I ignore the flurry of activity to my right and methodically pull the shell apart at the legs, then extract the shrimp from its tail. Next, I take the knife and slit the back of the shrimp to devein it. I don't know why they call it deveining shrimp, because the black line isn't really a vein. It's the shrimp's digestive tract, filled with poop. I rinse my finished shrimp, holding it up for the audience to see, and reach for another. Only there isn't one.

I've finished just in time to watch Chef Wu snag the last shrimp with his two-pronged fork, chop the tail off with his knife, and quickly slit the back to flip the shrimp's intestine onto a paper towel with it. He then slides the knife under the shell and peels it back to extract the meat with his fork.

I shake my head. "Show-off."

"This only a half-hour show," he says, grinning at the audience. They obey the laugh sign that lights up. He moves the shrimp to the side and pulls over the scallions. "Maybe I chop these while you get eggs from the cooler." He's a flurry of motion again, and I throw up my hands and mouth "yikes" for the cameras and audience, which draws only a few titters. What? They can't light up the laugh sign for me?

I turn on the burner to heat the wok, then go to the cooler to get eggs. A big chunk of butter reminds me that I like to cook in butter because it's low in carbs and has good fat that keeps you from getting hungry. Back at the wok, I throw some butter into the wok, then crack three eggs into a bowl and whisk.

"Cut!"

"Shit!" When I look up from my whisking to see why they're stopping the cameras, black smoke is billowing from the wok. I throw a nearby dish cloth over it, which catches fire before Chef Wu reaches down to turn off the burner. Someone rushes over with a fire extinguisher and puts the fire out, but not before the audience and camera crew are coughing.

"What did you put in my wok?" The *Wok-ee* chef is not pleased, and his accent has reverted from Asian to Southern.

"Nothing. Just butter. That's what I always scramble my eggs in."

"Your Teflon frying pan does not heat as quickly and as hot as a wok." He jerks his hat off his head and fans the smoke away from him before stomping off. "I'll be in my dressing room while you get this cleared up," he tells the floor manager. Studio staff are already ushering the audience out into fresh air, while others are wheeling in big fans to clear out the smoke.

I just stand there for a long minute, then hear a staff member telling the last of the audience being herded outside that they can expect to reenter in about twenty minutes. So, I give my destination to the floor manager and head for the green room shared by several shows in the building.

❖

Apparently, several cooking shows are taping today because I'm not the only guest star in a chef's jacket. I recognize a comedian from a show based in New York City getting something from the room's buffet, and he holds up a bottle of water in a questioning gesture. I nod, and he brings it to me.

"Hey. You're that actor they killed off in *Judge and Jury*, aren't you?" he asks.

"Yeah."

"I know it doesn't feel like it now, but it's probably the best thing that will ever happen to you career-wise. Being on one show too long can destroy your career when the show ends. The fans will never see you as anybody other than that character you played for years."

I hadn't thought of this angle. I can spin my dismissal as me wanting to avoid being typecast. In fact, I can go with that now. "That's exactly why I asked them to get rid of me. I want to return to my roots and do theater." As the words flow from my lips, my heart recognizes the truth. I do want to go back to acting onstage, where the audiences are real and the reviews written by professionals, not any goober who can post a blog.

He laughs. "You keep saying that until you believe it, too. Everybody knows why you're doing cooking shows now."

"Fuck." My Lisa debacle—my name for the unfortunate incident—is going to be hard to live down professionally.

"Yeah. Sleep-and-tell can be career suicide. You'll have to give it some time and lay low for a while."

"Maybe I should try to break into theater in London."

His laugh turns into a cackle. "Honey, there are no bigger gossips than the London media. You think they won't dig up your LA crime? Think again." He stops laughing and waggles his eyebrows at me. "If you want to make your downtime interesting, my girlfriend is considering a threesome, and you look like her type."

Straight men are all the same. I put down my bottle of water. "Sorry. I should go check to see if they're ready for me on set." I exit the green room in long strides. If I'm going to be burned, I'd rather it be while attempting to cook.

❖

The set still reeks, but the fans have eliminated the smoke well. The staff is ushering the audience back in, and Chef Wu is back at his cooking station. He has cleared away my stuff for shrimp fried rice and set out the ingredients for his surprise dish. He doesn't even look my way when I stand next to him behind the cooking island.

"Rolling cameras in five, four, three, two." The floor manager points to us, indicating the cameras are live.

Chef Wu looks at me and grins. "Look like shrimp fried rice go up in smoke." His broken-English-and-Asian accent is back. He cackles a laugh, and the audience joins in when the laugh sign lights up. "We cook my dish now," he says when the sign goes dark and the laughter stops.

He shuffles my way and elbows me to move two feet to my left so he is standing in front of the ingredients that he begins to name for the audience. "We have bean sprouts, baby carrots, scallions, peppers. Other ingredients are for sauce."

I nod because I think I should be contributing something.

"While Davis chop up some ingredients, I prepare sauce."

He begins to rattle off the ingredients as he puts them in the bowl but pauses when he sees I'm still standing motionless. "Chop, chop." He points to the peppers and onion, then takes the onion and begins slicing, then chopping the few slices he's cut—all with lightning speed. "Chop, chop." He puts the knife in my hand and returns to making the sauce.

I start slicing and dicing, glad he's already cored and cleaned the bell peppers to get rid of the seeds. My eyes water a bit from the onions, but I manage to chop all but the smaller red peppers. Then I gallantly begin to dice them and flick away the few seeds inside with my finger but make the mistake of wiping my eye still watering from the onion. Suddenly, my eye is on fire. MY EYE IS ON FIRE. "Motherfucker. Motherfucker."

"Cut!"

Chef Wu grabs me by the neck and forces me over to the sink, where he pushes my head in and grabs a carton of milk that a staff member hands him. The milk takes the edge off my pain, but when I open my eyes, I nearly faint at the blood mingling with the milk before it goes down the drain. "Oh my God! Is my eye bleeding?"

Chef Wu whispers in my ear. "No. Your finger is bleeding. You must have cut it when you got the pepper juice in your eye. You're not supposed to chop the small peppers. They go in the stir-fry whole." He returns to the cooking table while a staffer tends to my wounds.

"Rolling cameras in five, four, three, two." And we're back. I have a patch over one eye, and my finger is wrapped up like a cigar in a huge white bandage.

Chef Wu bows to me but doesn't try to hide his smile. "My apologies. Red pepper very hot. Do not chop or touch eyes before washing hands very good."

He turns back to the audience. "Everything ready now, so it time to bring out our surprise ingredient." He reaches under the cook top and pulls out a large bowl of…something that has legs. "Baby octopus," he says. "These in the bowl already prepared for stir-frying, but…" He reaches below again and retrieves a covered tray. "I have extra one we let Davis show you how to prepare."

I stare down at the tray and the helpless baby octopus, barely aware Chef Wu is slipping my damaged hand into a nitrile glove.

"Take tenacles in one hand and use other to pull head off," he says, handing it to me.

My stomach does a slow roll. "It's not still alive, is it?"

"Not after you pull head off." He laughs hilariously, and the audience joins in.

I can't even look to see if they're really laughing or obeying the sign. I'm staring at the unfortunate ocean creature, telling myself this is no different from calamari, which I love to eat. It's like pulling the head off a shrimp or a crawfish, right? Wrong. This one has a bulbous head shaped like all those early aliens I saw in the movies when I was a kid. What if I was beheading a sentient being?

"Very dead," Chef Wu says. "Been in ice for two days. Pull head off."

I close my one exposed eye and yank. The head comes off cleanly, but my stomach does another roll when he instructs me to pull the skin off the head, then reach in and jerk everything inside the head out—like emptying a sack. I swallow down my stomach contents that are trying to crawl up my esophagus and strip the skin from the legs as well.

"Since this baby octopus, we leave bottom half intact. On big octopus, we cut legs free. Oh, and check to make sure beak is removed." I let out a breath of relief when he takes it from my hand and demonstrates where to look for the beak. "Now we soak overnight in milk to tenderize tentacles."

I easily slip into assistant role as Chef Wu begins his stir-fry. He finishes quickly because the floor manager is indicating our time is running out, then grabs some chopsticks and samples the stir-fry.

"Delicious, spicy," he declares.

I'm smiling at the camera and pulling off the nitrile glove, so I don't see his chopsticks laden with octopus coming my way. I turn to him to say something, and he pops the octopus into my mouth.

Don't spit it out. Don't spit it out. I chew furiously, but I can't get the entire thing in my mouth. Chef Wu is waving good-bye at the camera, so I turn and wave, too.

"And cut!"

CHAPTER SIX

No more cooking shows, Kylie. I mean it."
       "Oh my God. You were spectacular. The episode aired yesterday, and the views on the internet are already a million above their all-time high for any episode. The show wants to know if they can negotiate to print and sell a poster of that final frame where you're standing next to Chef Wu with that huge bandage on your hand, another bandage on your eye, and octopus legs hanging out of your mouth while you wave good-bye."

I cover my eyes and groan. "No. Absolutely not."

"I'll email you their proposal. When you see the amount of money you'll make, you might want to reconsider."

"No." I don't have much time to talk because Mom has just signed all her discharge papers and I'm retrieving the car while someone wheels her down to the patient pick-up door. "What else do you have for me?"

"A couple of offers for commercials, but you don't want them."

"Try me," I say. What could be worse than chewing on octopus? I'm thinking of Jennifer Garner promoting a credit card or Charles Barkley selling potato chips.

"One is for female incontinence. Another is for vodka, which I don't think would be good for your career, considering alcohol got you in trouble to begin with."

I don't even hear the second opportunity. My brain is still tripping over the first. "Female incontinence? Really? How old do they think I am?"

"It's not like that. They're marketing their panty liners to a younger crowd...stay fresh all day."

"That's a hard no."

"There is a third offer you might want to consider—an insurance company that will be shooting in New York. Are you okay working with animals?"

"Sure. I like animals. That one sounds good. Book it."

"Okay."

"Any theater offers?"

"I've put out some feelers, but nothing so far."

"Okay. Try a little harder on that front, okay?"

A few seconds of silence pass before she speaks again. She must be having a bad day because her tone is suddenly hard, like steel. "I have always worked hard for you, Davis."

"I'm just thinking maybe there's someone who has more contacts in the theater community."

"Nobody else is going to waste their time begging parts for you like I do."

My anger rises to meet her pissed-off tone. "That's what I'm talking about. How can you be doing your best to represent me with an attitude like that?"

"You know what? I'll represent you for the commercial, but then you can find yourself a new agent."

"Fine." My retort disappears into dead air because Kylie has already disconnected the call. "Fine," I say aloud to myself. I'll give her several days to cool off, and then I'll call her again.

I stuff my phone into my pocket and pull into the hospital roundabout where you pick up patients. Mom is already there, sitting in a wheelchair while a candy-stripe volunteer who brought her down scrolls on her phone and vapes. Still irritated by my argument with Kylie, I slam to a stop and jump out of my car.

"Excuse me. I'm sure it's against hospital policy for you to vape next to a patient who just had surgery."

The girl stares at me, her expression disdainful. "I'm outside. We're allowed to smoke and vape outside. Besides, vaping isn't harmful like secondhand cigarette smoke is."

"And what doctor told you that?"

"I saw it on YouTube."

"It's okay, honey. We were only here for a minute," Mom says.

I snatch the teen's phone from her hands, find her Chrome app, and google "Is second-hand vape harmful?" Then I show her the array of studies that explain how vaping aerosols leaves droplets of harmful chemicals in the air that can be breathed in or absorbed through the skin or stick to surrounding objects. It is especially dangerous around toddlers, who might touch surfaces covered with these droplets, then put their hands into their mouths.

I quickly transfer a third load of flowers to my car and then glare at her when she looks up from her reading. "You shouldn't volunteer in a hospital if you aren't interested in people's health."

She tokes on her vape pen again, blowing the vapor upward, and smirks. "Didn't volunteer. I was sentenced to this as community work for drag racing."

"Huh. I see you're just full of smart decisions." I help Mom into my car and pause before closing her door. "Take my advice and give up things that can hurt you and the people around you."

I close Mom's door, and I'm walking around the car to get in the driver's side when the teen laughs. "Like you're somebody to be giving out advice."

I falter. *What the hell?*

"Yeah. I know who you are. You fucked up so bad, they killed you off the show."

The little bitch. "Grow up and get your news from adult sources, not stupid teen bloggers. My character was killed because I quit to take another offer. I didn't want to be another

Lucy Lawless who'll only ever be known for her Xena role." I slam the car door and peel out of the hospital parking lot.

Mom is quiet while I pull onto the street and wait at the next red light.

"So, who licked the red off your candy today?"

"I'd like to slap the red off that candy striper. The last thing you need after surgery is her secondhand vape going into your lungs."

She's quiet again until we reach home and I help her into bed, then bring in her dozen vases of flowers and place them around the house.

"They said your insurance is sending a home health nurse over in a little bit to show us how you should climb out of bed and get around until your back heals some."

"Okay, dear. Bryan has already made my bathroom handicap friendly, but could you put the walker next to my bed?"

"Nope. If I leave it there, you'll try to get up by yourself. Here's your phone. You can text me if I'm not in this room and you need the bathroom, and I'll bring the walker to you after I help you out of bed. Do you need something for pain? I've already filled your prescriptions."

"You're so sweet. They gave me pain medication right before you picked me up." She smiles up at me and pats the bed next to her. "Now sit right here and tell me why you're so angry before those pills put me to sleep."

"That kid was stupid to be vaping right next to you. What was she thinking?"

"Come on, now. What did she mean when she said you shouldn't be giving out advice?"

I huff out a breath and avoid her gaze. "She's just been reading those stupid, sensationalizing gossip blogs. People reporting that stuff have no credentials or ethics. They can print anything they want to make up on the internet and get away with it."

"So, tell me the truth about you quitting the show. And don't lie to your mother."

I stare at my hands. Mom knows I'm gay, so there's no condemnation there, but I don't want to see the disappointment in her eyes when I tell her how I behaved. "How much do you know?"

"I wouldn't look at the videos the gossips at the beauty shop kept trying to show me. But from what I gather, you embarrassed one of your costars and had to quit the show because of it."

"That's pretty much the gist."

"How about giving me a few more of the details?"

"I'd been dating Lisa Langston for several months, and we slept together enough to be a couple. But a huge birthday party was thrown for her, and she spent the night on Charleigh Long's lap. She didn't even have the decency to break up with me. So, I got drunk and picked up an attractive woman, who turned out to be paparazzi and got me on camera ranting about Lisa. When she posted it online, I basically outed Lisa."

"Oh, Davis."

"It wasn't my fault that woman videoed me while I was drunk."

"Whose fault was it that you were drunk?"

"Lisa's. We were together, and she was fawning all over this other woman right in front of me. I was hurt because I was in love with her."

Her nod is more an acknowledgment of the information than an agreement that I was guiltless. "That happened more than a month ago. Why were you mad when you pulled up to get me today? And don't say it was because that teenager was vaping. Your face was full of anger."

Geez. Moms sure know how to get into your stuff. "I had a fight with Kylie on the phone when I was walking out to the car."

"With Kylie? Whatever about?"

"She keeps bringing me crap offers like that stupid cooking show."

Mom chuckles. "You were adorable on that show. I've never laughed so hard. I loved the way they edited it so you could hear that guy yell 'cut!' Then they come back with everything cleaned up, but you have an eye patch and a huge bandage on your finger."

I scowl at her. "Keep it up, and I'll dump you at Bryan's house."

"No. Please don't do that. I desperately want to sleep in my own bed." I place a glass of sweet tea on her bedside table, but she picks it up and takes a few sips. "So, why are you angry with Kylie today?"

"She called me with some stupid commercial jobs. Female incontinence. Can you believe that?"

"It's a real problem that women don't talk about enough."

I ignore her observation because I refuse to even talk about the issue. "I want to get back on the stage, Mom. I've always loved theater. I've told Kylie that's what I want, and she brings me cooking shows and commercials."

"Give her some time, honey. You just finished with that TV show."

"I haven't gotten a good paycheck in almost three months."

"Where did all your money go?"

"They shut down production for two weeks until Lisa's people could lie their way out of her being a lesbian, and then they sued me for the money they lost during the weeks they weren't shooting. It pretty much drained me."

"Didn't you get paid to be on that cooking show?"

"That didn't go far after Kylie and Uncle Sam got their cut, and I used most of it to pay off the credit cards I've been living on." I slump into Mom's recliner that's been moved from the living room to her bedroom.

"I've got a good bit saved up. I can make you a loan," Mom says.

"Thanks, but Kylie has an offer for me to film a commercial for an insurance company. I told her I'd do it, and then I'm looking for an agent who has better contacts in the theater community."

Mom stares at me for a long moment. "You're firing Kylie? You girls have been friends since high school."

"This is business, Mom. This is my career."

"When one door closes, another always opens, Davis. But when you lose a good friend like Kylie, there's not always another who will know you as well or who you can trust as much."

❖

I slip into the theater and sit in the semidarkness of the back row, Mom's rebuke still stinging. Kylie's email was terse, listing the date, time, and place for the commercial shoot, along with a link to a contract for me to sign. Then I called a handful of agents who represent actors currently on and off Broadway, but none returned my calls. I felt cold inside and needed to lose myself in the warmth of this familiar place, this stage where I learned to act.

Asia is up there with Tommy, the female lead, and the male lead. Tommy is reading the priest's lines, and the others are arguing over the upcoming holidays. They go through their lines, but the female actor is shaking her head at the tone and body language Asia wants.

"Just try it the way I'm suggesting," Asia says.

The girl actually tosses her hair and puts her hand on her hip. "I'm not seeing it. I'm playing it like I feel my character would."

I put my hand over my mouth to hide my smirk. If a rookie actor spoke to a seasoned director in that tone, she'd be shown the exit before she could draw another breath.

Tommy spots me and gives a little wave, and then Asia looks up and sees me, too. Her three actors keep their eyes on her as she paces the length of the stage and back, then waves me down from the seats to the stage.

I'm so surprised, I glance to either side of me for some other person she might be beckoning, then point to myself and mouth "me?" She nods and waves for me to come down.

My heart does a little happy dance, but I try to maintain my outward cool and saunter to her. Static electricity lifts her hair up on the sides when she runs her hands through it in a frustrated gesture. Her hazel eyes are gray under the stage lights, and I've never seen a woman more beautiful. "What's up?"

"Davis, this is Sonya and Trey," she says, then points at me. "Davis is a professional actor." She puts a big emphasis on "professional."

Sonya gives me a bored look, which says she doesn't have a clue who I am, but Trey leers like he watches my previous show and has read all the gossip.

Asia takes Sonya's script and hands it to me. "Could you help us out by reading Rebecca's lines in this scene?"

"Sure."

"Great. Okay. Rebecca is arguing with Michael over whether their son should be christened. She's not entirely sure of her side of the argument at first, but she becomes more adamant as Michael grows more resolute."

I scan the pages she has marked. "Can we run through it once, so I can get a feel for it?"

She nods. "Let's start with her telling Father Tim that since they didn't circumcise their son in keeping with Jewish tradition, they aren't going to christen him to satisfy her in-laws' Catholic faith."

Trey—despite his frat-boy leer—turns out to be a pretty good actor, and we easily fall into the back-and-forth of the dialogue. When we finish, Asia is nodding.

"Good, good. I just have a few suggestions." She asks Trey and me both for a few adjustments I feel are good corrections, then claps her hands together. "Let's try it again."

We run through the scene again, and she turns to Sonya when we finish. "Did you see how Davis played that?"

Sonya nods, her previous attitude gone. "Yeah. I can do that."

I return Asia's script and offer Sonya a little advice. "This is a good script. If you want to play something a different way, ask

Asia's permission to show her. But in the end, she's the director and can replace actors who refuse her vision of the script."

The girl at least has the graciousness to blush. "Got it."

Asia looks surprised at my reprimand and Sonya's suddenly meek acceptance. "Thanks, Davis. I appreciate your help. That's a wrap for today, guys. I'll see Trey and Sonya back here tomorrow to read the Hanukkah scene."

They gather their coats and backpacks clustered downstage and head for the back exit. I walk with Asia to the control room. Tommy trails a few discreet feet behind us.

"What are you doing in my theater on this random afternoon?" She gives me a hard stare, but I can see the corner of her mouth twitching upward in a tiny smile.

"Because I like it when you order me out?" I start to slide into my cocky Davis, but I'm suddenly overcome with an emotion that's foreign to me—the need to be honest. I want her to see me, not a role I'm playing. I stop smiling. "Actually, I'm a little rudderless and beat up right now." I sweep my arm to indicate the theater outside the glass booth. "Theater, this one in particular, is like home and a healing elixir to me. I came here this afternoon for the comfort of something familiar."

Tommy has joined us in the booth and is nodding his understanding. He gives me a one-arm hug that I lean into. "We practically grew up in this building, didn't we?"

Asia studies us, and I nod. Tommy gets me. At times, I wonder if Bruce was the only reason he returned to Christmas. This theater was a second lover he couldn't leave in a quest for fame.

"I can't pay you because I can't afford guild rates. If you'll consider some volunteer work, I could use some help coaching the young actors and keeping the understudies up to speed. The grant that's supporting this production is bogging me down with paperwork—weekly reports and financial accounting. I pretty much have to justify every pen I buy."

My thoughts are a chaotic mosh pit. I'll get to see her almost every day. I'll get to feel the stage beneath my feet and run lines with other actors. I can breathe in the smell of old wood, dust burning off the hot stage lights, and stale popcorn. I will sweep Asia off her feet in just a couple of weeks. Yes! My old mojo is coming back. I slip back into my familiar cocky Davis role. "I'm interested. How about I take you to dinner, and we can iron out the details?" I offer her my smile that I've practiced enough in the mirror to know it shows off my dimples.

Her expression instantly changes, and she looks at me like I'm something she needs to scrape off the bottom of her shoe. "On second thought, forget it." She flips the switches to kill the stage lights and begins packing up her messenger bag.

"What? You don't eat dinner?"

She stops stuffing papers into her bag and glares at me. "This play is very important to me and to this community. If we draw a good audience, the tourists will eat in the local restaurants and shop in the local gift stores. I don't have time for your games or to build up your enormous ego. I thought for a moment that you truly wanted to help. My mistake." Then she closes her bag. "Please, don't follow me out. I don't want to have dinner or coffee with you…ever." Then she stalks away.

I'm stunned.

"Burn," Tommy says.

I turn to him. "What the hell happened? She's hot and cold, sweet then sour."

"Dude." Tommy shoots me a disgusted stare, shaking his head. "You can't keep that dog on a leash, can you?"

"I don't know what you're talking about."

"She wants to work with you, but the minute she offered to let you in, you reverted to that I-want-to-get-in-your-pants Davis."

"Who wouldn't want to get in her pants? She's gorgeous. And tell me you don't feel the gay vibes coming off her."

His disgust hardens into a scowl, so I try a different tactic.

"I was being charming, offering to buy her dinner and talk about the cast."

"You're hopeless." His scowl softens.

I shake off his accusation. "Do you want to go grab something to eat somewhere?"

"No. I'm going home to eat with my husband. I'd invite you over, but you should go home and make dinner for your mother, who just had surgery."

"Yeah, okay. I'm going." We kill the remaining lights and walk into the sunlit lobby. "So, does this mean she doesn't want me to help now?"

He stops to lock the doors after we step out onto the plaza, then turns to me and cocks his head in a sarcastic-queen classic move. "You think?"

❖

My phone dings with a text message from a number I don't recognize.

This is Phil Tessio. Your account has been shifted from Kylie to me. What's your email address?

What the hell? Apparently, Kylie's agency has assigned a new agent to me. I don't like it, but I decide to go with it since I haven't had any luck finding an agent on my own. I text back my email addy, then take a tray holding Mom's dinner to the bedroom.

"Thank you, sweetie." Mom is propped up in bed with about twenty pillows I've stuffed behind her back. "It smells so good."

"It's Mrs. Zymbowski's chicken soup. You were still napping when she brought it over." I lay a towel over her chest to catch any drips. "I know how you love naan bread, so I picked this up fresh from Main Street Bakery."

"You're taking such good care of me." She pats my arm.

"Now, set up a TV tray by my recliner and bring your dinner in here. We can watch *Jeopardy* and *Wheel of Fortune* together like we used to."

I do as she asks because we love to see who can get the correct answer first and shout our guesses at the television. *Jeopardy* has always been my favorite. I dominate in showbiz and sports categories, and I'm pretty good at geography. Mom aces science, art, and history categories. After I take our dinner trays to the kitchen, we watch a family drama Mom likes. Well, Mom watches, and I mentally sort through my insecurities.

"Mom. What if I don't get another acting job? Not bit pieces. I mean another role on a hit show or a movie?"

These are doubts I can reveal only to her, because she knows the little girl inside me. Even as I ask, I stare at the television. I can't bear for her to see how scared I am deep inside. When she doesn't answer, I glance over at her bed and realize she's sound asleep. I turn off the television, then go to her to adjust her pillows and pull her blanket up like she doubtlessly did so many times for Bryan and me when we were kids.

I don't really know how to take care of somebody. Because I was the baby in the family, everybody took care of me. But being home has reminded me how much I love my mom. So, I pack my bag for a one-night stay in New York City, grab a blanket and my laptop, then get comfortable in the recliner next to her bed in case she wakes up and needs pain medicine or help getting to the bathroom.

The email from my new agent is in my inbox, and I push aside any guilt I'm feeling for going to New York the next day. I've had to ask her best friend to sit with Mom during the day until Bryan gets off work and comes over to spend the night.

The email my agent has sent has no warm introduction, no "happy to be working with you" or "I'm working some good leads for you," just my travel information with a note that he'll pick me up at the Amtrak station. I don't know why he didn't just text that to me.

I close my email, which is nothing but a lot of junk, and venture where no performer or author should go. I google myself to see what bloggers are writing about me now. The show's episode about my character's demise has aired several weeks before, but almost three months have passed, and I'm hoping at least some of the chatter will be about missing me. I click through some blogs that follow the show, and my ego shrivels at the comments from readers.

Good riddance, traitor.

Glad Lisa's safe from that pathetic liar.

She's a lesbian's worst nightmare—that ex-girlfriend who spreads your shit out for everyone to see. The drunk bitch should be in rehab.

That lezzie is just a delusional stalker, drooling over her straight costar.

Now I'm angry. I'm not the only lesbian who ever got drunk when a lover stomped on her feelings. If that blogger had written the truth about how Lisa treated me that night, those commenters would be on my side. I slam my laptop shut, and Mom stirs at the noise.

She stays still for a long moment, but I can see her eyes blink open because light is shining in from her bathroom. "Davis?"

"I'm here, Mom. Are you hurting? Do you need your medicine?"

She tries to roll onto her side toward me, and I jump up to help her. Her voice is tight and a little shaky. "A little, but I need to go to the bathroom."

"Hold on. Let me get your walker, and then I'll help you up." We shuffle to the bathroom, and I have to help her pull her panties down, then up again after she's finished peeing. Ugh. Parts of your parent you never expected to have to see. I check her bandage and wait while she brushes her teeth. We shuffle back to the bed just in time. She's so spent from the effort that her hands shake when she accepts the cup of water to wash down her night medicines and some pain pills. When did she start taking blood pressure medicine? How much more have I missed because I never came home?

I flew her out to LA for the holidays the first year, but she has since celebrated the holidays with my brother's family. He has children, Santa Claus, snow, and mulled wine. It isn't my fault my poolside Christmas doesn't compare. I ruminate over having missed so many warm holiday moments with her, and I'm surprised to discover I have no memories saved from my LA holidays, which are a mere string of forgettable parties and hangovers.

I study her features in the dim illumination of the bathroom's night light and whisper, "I love you, Mom."

Again, I'm surprised when she answers back. "I love you, too, my sweet girl."

Not so sweet, according to Asia. Damn it. Why does she keep popping up in my head?

CHAPTER SEVEN

I'm searching the Amtrak terminal crowd for a guy—probably in a business suit—holding up a sign with my name on it when a grizzled old man wearing huge, thick glasses and a cardigan sweater with his pants pulled high on his protruding stomach like Rudy Giuliani and carrying a battered briefcase walks up.

"I'm Phil Tessio. Follow me."

I hold out my hand. "I'm Davis Hart." I want to make sure he knows he has the right person.

"I know who you are." He ignores my hand and takes off in a fast walk.

I'm irritated by his abrupt non-greeting because I woke up this morning with a case of menstrual cramps, and my last dose of Midol is wearing off. "Maybe I have a checked bag to retrieve."

He stops and turns to me. "You're here for one night. You needed more than a carry-on?"

"No, but you didn't ask." I follow, grumbling under my breath, when he resumes walking. "It's true that New Yorkers have no manners."

"I don't have time to be polite," he says, his gaze fixed on the door leading to the outdoor taxi queue. Damn, he's fast for a guy who looks to be a hundred years old.

He stuffs us into a cab and gives rapid directions to the warehouse district near the Brooklyn waterfront before setting his briefcase on his knees and shuffling through it. When he finds the papers he wants, he closes the briefcase and slides it onto my lap with the papers and a pen on top. "This is the standard contract, except that it's for only three months, with an option for another three."

I hesitate, glancing over the writing. "Why only three months?"

"Because I'm retired and taking you on to repay a favor. That's how showbiz works. It's a world run on favors. You do me a favor, then I do you one later."

"Why do I need to sign with you to do this commercial? Kylie's already set it up, so she gets the commission."

"If you have to know, she's paying me to walk you through this, then put feelers out for a Broadway role for you."

My ears prick up at this. "You live here in the city?"

"My whole life."

"So, you have contacts in the theater community?"

He lowers his chin to glare at me over the top of his glasses, which have migrated down his nose. "What's the longest-running show ever on Broadway?"

"*Phantom of the Opera.*" I answer quickly. I've seen *Phantom* three times on Broadway.

He nods and pushes his glasses back into place. "If you'd answered anything else, I'd tear up that contract and leave you at this two-bit commercial gig." He slaps his knee. "Of course I have contacts in theater. I've been an agent in this city for nearly fifty years."

I scribble my signature quickly on the contract and shove his briefcase back to him. "Look, I know I've literally screwed my chances in LA, but my roots are in theater. I love it and want to try to get a fresh start there."

"None of that LA hanky-panky here."

I hold up three fingers in a Girl Scout salute and then cross my heart. "Absolutely. I just want to work." It's an easy promise to make since the cramping in my lower belly is escalating.

He slaps my knee this time. "Good."

The cab stops outside a warehouse that has been converted to house a half dozen photography sets. He leads me to one in the back and goes over to talk to the guy ordering everyone around.

I walk up to a woman, who appears to be part of the staff, and hold up my Midol. "Is there a bathroom around here, and maybe some water?"

She grimaces in solidarity with my suffering and points to the left corner. "You'll find a ladies' changing room with a bathroom over there. I'll have a bottle of water for you when you come back."

"Thanks." I give her a grateful look and hurry off, wheeling my overnight bag with me.

When I return, she hands me a bottle of water and takes my bag. "I'll put this over there with my stuff. Nobody will bother it. I'm Sarah, by the way."

"Davis." I down the pills but keep the water. "Is there a place I can sit until they're ready to shoot?"

"Sure. Sit in any of those studio chairs over by the cameras. It shouldn't be long. The animal trainer is out back, where they're going to shoot first." She walks me to the chairs, and I wrap my long overcoat around me before sinking into the nearest one. "I'll come get you when they're ready to start shooting. In the meantime, give me a wave if you need anything else."

I thank her again as two guys and a woman walk over. All are wearing business suits and introduce themselves as representing the advertising agency. The taller guy hands me a one-page script.

"These are your lines. Can you read them to us so I can correct your inflection or any mispronounced words?"

I look at him. Right away, I don't like this guy. He's smug and obviously controlling. I hold the script out to him. "You read them like you envision the commercial, so I can get an idea of the tone you want."

He smirks. "It's only a simple paragraph. We need to get it in two or three takes because the attention span of your animal costars is limited."

I'm on the verge of going all she-wolf on him, but I take a deep breath and stand up because I can tell I'm taller than he is. I step close and look down on him. "You seem like the kind of guy that likes correcting women, but I'm being paid union rates by the hour for this little job and don't want to waste your agency's money. This will go quicker if you show me what you want rather than me guessing and letting you correct me."

"That sounds good, Ms. Hart," the other guy says as both men back up a step.

Mr. Smug clears his throat and reads the script, then hands it to me. His reading was awful, so I scan it and do my own version. He's shaking his head, but the woman and the second guy are nodding.

"That's even better," the second guy says. "Way better than your read, Ray."

The woman, who hasn't spoken yet, is nodding vigorously.

"Whatever," Ray says, then walks away.

Sarah has returned. "We're ready for you, Davis."

We step into bright sunlight that is no match for the cold front that has swept into the city. Smug guy is back at my elbow.

"Sorry, but you'll have to lose the coat. We want people all over the country to relate to our commercial, not just the ones in the cold states."

Phil appears suddenly on the other side of me. "She keeps her coat on until the moment they're ready to roll camera," he says.

Smug guy shrugs and walks away.

I notice Phil's ears are red from the cold. "Where's your coat, Phil?"

"Ahh. My wife call you or something? I left it and my hat at home. It's not that bad out."

But I can tell he's cold, so I gesture for Sarah to come over. "Hey. I notice you guys are all wearing knit caps with your production company logo. Any more of those around?"

"Mitch always has a couple extra in his backpack in case

some of the staff forget theirs and a shoot turns cold on us," she says. "How many do you need?"

"Just one," I say, pointing to Phil's ears.

She smiles. "Coming right up."

I like this woman in a friend kind of way. When she returns with the cap, I ignore Phil's protest as I pull it over his head. "Don't make me call your wife and tell her you didn't bring your coat."

He chuckles at my threat but leaves the hat pulled down over the tips of his ears. Then we watch as they run two chimpanzees through crashing two golf carts into each other. After that, one hops out and lies on the ground while the other chimp holds his head in dismay and pounds on the front of the cart where it's supposedly damaged. That's when I walk onto the scene, hand the distraught chimp a check, then help the injured chimp up and place a sling on his arm.

"At Farm and City Insurance, we don't monkey around when you've been in an accident. Nobody beats our rates or our customer service."

I've seen better amateur videos on TikTok. But it's the kind of stupid commercial guys would like.

They're ready to shoot, so everything rewinds. The crew attaches fake hoods and bumpers that will crumple as though the carts were traveling at a higher speed, and I get ready to step in and read my stupid lines. "Hold my coat for me, will you?" It nearly touches the ground when I drape it over Phil's shoulders rather than handing it to him.

He doesn't protest. "Sure, sure. I gotcha."

The chimps and I run through the commercial flawlessly until the end, when I stand up to say my lines after putting the sling on the second chimp and the first chimp swings around and buries his nose in my crotch.

"Cut," the director yells.

I struggle to push the chimp away, but he persists until his trainer comes over with a collar and leash and drags him away.

"What the fuck?"

The second chimp shrinks back when I yell at the male trainer, and his female assistant picks her up to comfort her. "It's okay, Lola. She's not mad at you." She speaks in a low, soothing voice, and it takes a moment for me to realize she's edging toward me. "Could you just tell her in a quiet voice that you're not mad with her?" I realize the assistant didn't vary her tone or volume so the crew would think she was still talking to the chimp.

I like animals, so I comply. Actually, I'm willing to do anything to hurry this shoot up and go back inside where it's warmer. "I didn't mean to scare you, sweetie." I stroke her head. "I'm a little scared of your buddy, though, since he decided to molest me on camera."

Keeping the same tone, the assistant touches my arm to guide me toward their equipment trailer. "I'm guessing that you must be on your period?"

I scowl. "Is that why Bobo molested me?"

"He's a male chimp. We'll have to reschedule the shoot. We don't have a female replacement for him."

"I'm only here for one day."

She hesitates, then leads me behind their trailer, out of sight of everybody else. "There is one thing we can do, if you're willing."

I shiver, since the only thing between me and the cold is my silk shirt. "Anything if it means we can get this over with and go back inside."

She pulls out one of those herbal pouches you heat in a microwave, then place on a sore joint or muscle. "He hates the smell of the herbs in this. I have to use it when I'm having my period to keep him away. Just stuff it down in your pants."

I blink a few times. Did she just tell me to…? For the first time, I give her a good look. She has an athletic build and definite gay vibes. I glance at the pouch. She's had this stuffed in her pants before? A slight breeze prompts me to shiver again. What the hell? I take the pouch and shove it in my underwear because my slacks are dressy and loose, and I don't want it sliding down my pants leg at an inopportune time. Besides, I don't have a problem touching or tasting another woman's pussy, so why would I object to putting a pouch for her pussy next to mine? "Let's do this."

The second take is a wrap after Bobo takes one sniff at my crotch, loses all interest in me, and keeps his eyes on his trainer's hand signals.

The second commercial, apparently the brainchild of the woman copy writer, is fun. My pain meds are working, we're inside where it's warmer, and my costar is an adorable French bulldog.

I'm sitting yoga style on a plush rug with several auto policies spread out before me and my costar, Rollo, next to me.

"My car insurance company raised my rates again, even though I have a good driving record and no claims."

Rollo raises his cute face and howls.

"Exactly," I say, nodding to him. "So, we need to find a new company. How about this one?" I pick up the first policy, but Rollo snatches it from my hand and proceeds to rip it to shreds.

"Okay. Not that one," I say, then pick up a second policy. "This one looks better. They even provide a rental car while mine is being repaired after an accident."

Rollo howls again, then jumps up and races to a nearby table to retrieve a magnifying glass for me. He drops the glass in front of me and taps his paw on the fine print at the bottom of the policy. I pick up the glass and peer at what he's pointed out.

"Oh. They pay only five dollars a day." I lower the page and glass to look at him. "What kind of car can you rent for five dollars?"

He snorts and shakes his entire body like he's fresh from a bath. Then he jumps up and brings over a third policy. When I take it from him, he sits back and does that cute "wah-wah-wah" Frenchy-speak as if he's telling me something about the policy. I take a look at it.

"This is more like it. Full coverage, a rental car comparable to your own car, and a great rate. And there's no fine print with Farm and City Insurance." We high-five, and I do a few small celebratory sitting dance moves while Rollo does little twirls.

We do three takes, but I think they're all good.

"That's a wrap, people," the director says.

When I stand, I'm more exhausted than I'd realized and still a bit cold. When the assistant trainer comes over with Rollo's leash, I lean close to her ear. "If you give me a minute to go to the changing room, I'll give the herbal pouch back to you."

She grins and keeps her voice low. "Keep it. After it being in your pants, it would probably bring a small fortune on eBay." She gives me a wink. "I wouldn't do that to you, but I don't trust that my money-grubbing wife wouldn't." She reaches down to slip the leash on Rollo, who's sniffing my pants leg.

I shake my head and smile. "Thanks for that, and for all your help today. Rollo is adorable."

We both look down at him, just in time to see him hike his leg and wet down my pants leg. I jump away, but I'm not quick enough.

"Bad Rollo." She scolds him as she picks him up. "I'm so sorry. He's never done that before. He must smell Bobo on your pants."

I drop my chin to my chest. A perfectly bad end to a bad day.

❖

Phil checks me in the Sheraton with a company credit card. "Tough day, kiddo, with that crazy monkey and that dog pissing on your pants. Go take a hot bath and order some room service for dinner. I happen to know their restaurant makes a great chicken soup or breakfast twenty-four hours, if that's what you want." He digs out his wallet and hands me his business card with his phone number. "Broadway parts aren't as plentiful as television roles, so give me a few weeks to see who's holding auditions.

Nothing new coming up right now, but actors sometimes get tired of working two shows a day and go back to television or movies, leaving a spot open. I'll call you." He jerks his thumb toward the front entrance. "Monty will pick you up in his cab at ten thirty tomorrow morning. He's already been paid and tipped to take you to the train."

I realize for the first time that the same guy was driving both times we've taken a cab that day, and he's waiting outside to take Phil home. "Monty. Right." I look at Phil. He's still wearing the knit cap, and it looks ridiculous with his hiked-up pants and cardigan sweater. Ridiculous and adorable. Damn hormones are making me emotional. I lunge forward and wrap him in a hug.

He gives me a quick squeeze, then pushes me away. "Enough. You stink of monkey and dog piss."

I grin. "You love me anyway."

"Yeah, yeah," he says over his shoulder as he walks away. "Good night, kiddo."

I reflect on the day as I ride up the elevator. Despite the animal mishaps, I've successfully shot one stupid commercial and one cute one in which I actually got to do a little acting. I want to call Kylie because she would laugh at my animal encounters. But I've fired her, and she hasn't spoken to me since. I haven't called or texted her either, but I've never been the one to give in first after we've had a tiff, and this feels more like a breakup than a tiff.

I pick up my phone, needing to feel less alone in my impersonal luxury-hotel room. I call my mom, but Bryan answers and says she's asleep. We make small talk for a few minutes, then end the call. My next effort to share my day with somebody is met by Tommy's voice mail. I realize he's probably at the theater, and my thoughts involuntarily jump to Asia.

Her intense, light-colored eyes capture me every time, but I'm starting to respect her decisiveness, her command of the stage, and her insight as a playwright. I just don't understand her resistance to me. We click when she lets me work with her onstage. I'm sure that's why she asked me to help with her actors, but I'm frustrated by her abrupt withdrawal. I can feel a chemistry between us, but every time I try to open that door, she slams it in my face.

I run a hot bath and mentally work on the puzzle that is Asia as I soak my body. When the water grows cold, I rise, dry off, and pull on the plush robe provided by the hotel. I order room service, build a backrest of pillows, and lie on the bed to wait. The TV remote is at my fingertips, but I don't reach for it. Instead, I savor my Asia-moments—static electricity fluffing her long, flowing curls as she stands under the stage lights, her confident coaching of the actors, and even the fire in her eyes when she glares at me. I slide my hand down against the throbbing between my legs, my fingers gliding in the thick lubrication. My cramps are threatening to return, so I decide to test the rumor that orgasms can relieve pain. I close my eyes, think of Asia, and stroke. Bare seconds pass before I convulse in climax, and my cramps evaporate as the aftershocks roll through me.

I'm limp when room service knocks at my door and am forced to rouse myself from a pleasant stupor. I hurriedly tip the server and rush them out so I can wash up. I'm starving and attack the food with gusto. Fifteen minutes later, my belly is pleasantly full and my resolve renewed. I will find a way back into that theater and next to the woman fueling my fantasies.

CHAPTER EIGHT

Mom's healing well and insists she can now manage the bathroom without help. I also discover that our neighbor, Mr. Healy, who's been widowed for two years, and Mom have been taking cooking classes at the community college. He's offered to come over to make dinner for them and keep her company until she's settled in for the night, leaving me free for the evening, so I'm off to wheedle my way back into Asia's production.

I cautiously push open the door between the lobby and auditorium only a crack and peek in. The actors appear to be taking a break while the crew changes the set. I'm thrilled to spot Ray, who Tommy said had become a recluse after his wife died, on the stage talking to Tommy and some other familiar actors. Apparently, several of the old Christmas Community Theater troupe won roles in the play. I open the door a little wider to see the inside of the lighting booth. Asia is talking with the costume mistress, Sadie, who has her sketchbook open. I watch them discuss Sadie's costume designs for a few more minutes, and then Sadie closes her sketchbook and seems to be wrapping up their discussion. Time to make my move.

I push my way through the door and into the lighting booth. "Hey, Sadie."

"Davis!" She wraps me in a big hug and kisses me on the cheek. "You old dog. What brings you back to Christmas?"

I decide to give her the short version, even though it's only a sidebar to the main reason. "Mom had back surgery, so I'm helping out at home." It's not a total lie.

I have two coffees in my hands and hold out one to Asia. "Since you seem to be a regular at the coffeehouse, I asked the barista to make your usual. I hope she got it right."

"Well, I've got to run," Sadie says, patting my shoulder. "Hope to see you around more."

I nod, still holding out the coffee that Asia accepts after a long hesitation, as Sadie exits.

"What are you doing here, Davis?" Asia removes the top from the cup and sniffs the brew. The coffee apparently passes her aroma test, and she takes a sip.

I decide truth is the best approach. "I'm bringing you apology coffee, hoping you'll reconsider and let me work with your actors—as a volunteer, of course." I hold up my go-to Girl Scout salute. "Just work. I promise to stop inviting you to dinner or to go out for coffee."

She studies me, but I refrain from giving her anything but my authentic expression. No acting. "Please. I just finished shooting a commercial in which I was peed on by a dog and nearly molested by a chimp that could smell I'm on my period. I need something to remind me what real acting is like."

Her expression is stoic. Then something sparks in her eyes, and her lips twitch. Suddenly, she bursts into a genuinely delighted laugh for the first time in my presence. I'm stunned. Not by her reaction, but at how beauty shines from her when she laughs so freely. I quickly school my expression to one of practiced embarrassment. If she sees how enamored I am, she'll throw me out again.

"Okay, okay," she says. "On a volunteer basis."

"Absolutely."

"And no flirting with me or any of the actors."

"Geez. That will be hard. Tommy is really cute. Have you ever seen him in a dress?"

She slaps at me with the script pages in her hand, then reaches for the table behind her and grabs me a full script of my own. "We're working on Act Two tonight."

I follow as she heads back down to the stage. The entire main cast is present—the two students playing the young couple, Rebecca and Michael, Ray as Rabbi Schwartz, Tommy as Father Finley, Susan as Michael's mother, and two other students playing Rebecca's parents. Understudies are hanging together downstage, ready to listen and take notes when we get started. Unless called up, they fill bit parts and act as extras in any scene that needs a crowd.

Asia claps her hands to get everyone's attention. "Guys, this is Davis Hart, for those who haven't met her yet. She's going to act as a consultant for the actors and specifically practice with the understudies to ensure they know their parts." In professional theater, the understudies don't get to actually practice the main acting roles. But community players aren't professional actors, so Asia is wisely taking extra measures to ensure the show will always go on. "Do you want to say anything, Davis, before we get started?"

"Some of you guys know me, but for those who don't, I grew up here in Christmas and spent my childhood watching the community players from those seats."

I point to the seating area. "When I was still a kid, I cut my acting teeth right here on this stage. This theater has a great tradition, and we're all hoping this production will pave the way for it to continue. So, I'm honored to be invited to help fight to keep these doors open."

My spiel is heartfelt, and Asia seems impressed. Even my ex-girlfriend Susan is nodding her agreement.

"Okay. Places, everyone, for Act Two," Asia says. "Let's read through it."

We spend the next two hours reading, blocking the actors' movements, and making notes. I haven't had this much fun in a long time.

❖

It's nearly eleven o'clock when I get home, still early by my usual LA standards. I'm a little disappointed that Mom is sound asleep and I can't tell her about my evening. I had a wonderful time sharing my commercial job experience with her earlier that afternoon before Mr. Healy came over to Mom-sit.

Mr. Healy. I'm shocked to see him still here, snoring up a storm in the recliner next to Mom's bed. I frown. I'm sure I made it clear he didn't have to stay until I got home. But he is an old man. He probably just fell asleep while they were watching TV. I gently shake his arm and call his name quietly. Mom stirs, but I'm unsure if it's the sound of my voice or the sudden absence of his loud snoring that wakes her.

"What time is it?" Mom rubs her eyes.

"A little after eleven."

Mr. Healy sits up in the recliner. "Gosh. I better go home."

"Thanks for hanging out with Mom tonight."

"I'm glad to do it every night you need to be at the theater." He smiles down at Mom. "We eat together several times a week anyway to try out recipes. It's no hardship to do it more often." He shakes his finger at her. "One day, I'm finally going to beat her at *Jeopardy.*"

"Not going to happen," Mom says. She's more awake now and pushes herself into a semi-sitting position.

He takes a step toward her, then stops when he glances at me. "Well, good night, ladies. I'll see myself out."

"How are things at the theater, honey?"

My heart instantly lifts, and my smile is wide. "I had a great time. I'm going to help coach the actors."

"Are you hungry? I know you didn't eat before you left."

"Starving."

"Al left a plate for you in the fridge. Go heat it up and bring it in here so you can tell me all about your evening."

While I warm my dinner, Mom hobbles to the bathroom, and then we both resettle in the bed and chair. The recliner is still faintly warm from Al's body heat, and a small seed of something nags at me. I frown, then shake my head, unable to put my finger on what's bothering me.

Mom looks a little pale after her excursion to the bathroom, so I open her pain pills and give her one. "Eat your dinner before it gets cold again," she says. "And tell me all about your night."

Chapter Nine

I watch, take notes, and video segments with my phone while Asia again runs her actors through the scene where Rebecca, played by Sonja, rants about the tug-of-war over the religion behind the approaching holidays while using her mother's maid, played by local actor Jean, as a sounding board. The dialogue is brilliant. Sonya constantly turns to Jean for advice, only to interrupt after Jean has spoken a few words or continues her tirade before Jean can speak at all.

When they reach the scene's end, Asia stands motionless for a moment, then shakes her head. "Something's not working." I clear my throat, and she turns to where I'm sitting in the front row of the auditorium. "Anything to offer?"

Okay. I have to walk a fine line between being helpful and sounding like she's an idiot not to see the problem. But directors usually do sit where I am—to get the audience's view of what's happening onstage. Community theater actors, however, often need more hands-on coaching, which is why Asia is on the stage with them.

I rise from my seat and join them. "I love this script. It's so Shakespearian." I begin cautiously, talking directly to the actors. Others not in this scene begin to gather downstage to listen, no doubt curious about my role on the staff. "It carries a serious message that while religions might seem different, their holidays are the same because they celebrate love and hope. But the play is written to be light-hearted family entertainment in keeping with the town's happy-holiday theme." I turn back to Asia. "Have I misunderstood?"

She shakes her head. "No. You're spot-on." She twirls her hand for me to continue.

I intend to be gentle, but Sonya is tapping at something on her Apple watch when I face her again, and I'm infuriated that she's the problem here and I don't have her full attention. I point to her. "Jean, who's playing her role perfectly, is totally upstaging you."

The older woman playing the maid has acted in this theater for years just for fun and offers only a slight nod and small smile to acknowledge my compliment. She wisely waits for me to correct the younger woman, who's being paid a stipend as the star of the show.

I dial it back a bit so I don't damage the young actor's confidence too much. "Your timing and dialogue are flawless, but you need to exaggerate your movements and expressions more. The people sitting on the back row and in the balcony pay to see the same play as those sitting in the front seats. So just pump it up a bit. Be more animated. Have fun with it." I look down at Asia, who's now sitting where I had been before. "Can we run through it again?"

"Yes. Places. Taking it from the top."

The redo isn't much better. Sonya is still too stiff, her acting too conservative. Mindful to avoid the impression that I'm taking over Asia's show, I hesitate. She apparently reads me perfectly.

"Davis, why don't you run the scene with Jean to show Sonya what you're talking about."

"Okay. I can do that." I'm suddenly, inexplicably self-conscious. I'm performing for Asia as well as Sonya. Jean gives me a wink, which helps me settle as we take our places to begin. I wait a heartbeat as everyone but Jean and me—Rebecca and the maid—fades from my consciousness. And, action.

I'm riding high when the scene concludes, buoyed by the

thrill of being onstage and stretching my acting wings again. The other actors applaud, and I take a mock bow. Thankfully, Sonya's nodding, her face alight with realization. Most of all, Asia is smiling and adding her own slow clap for my performance.

The rest of the rehearsal is amazing. After a bit of feeling our way, Asia and I begin to work in tandem to tweak the scenes and coach the actors. Everyone seems reluctant to stop when our stage manager notifies Asia it's already past eleven o'clock.

"Wow. Man, that was so much fun." Tommy is effusive, bumping my shoulder playfully. "We accomplished such a lot tonight."

"Theater is the best fun." I bump him back.

Asia's smile seems to signal her agreement. She cocks her head. "You didn't like working in television?"

"I do, but—" I pause to put words to my feelings. "Working on a TV set is so different. It feels more mechanical—cry or chase or argue with someone on demand. It's a lot of short, chopped-up scenes. The hardest thing for me to get used to was filming out of sequence. I mean, we jump from one scene to another in play rehearsal, but we at least usually make it through an entire scene, and sometimes several scenes in sequence."

"Your television experience must be why you can so easily switch from one role to a different one to demonstrate improvements for the actors."

I warm under her praise. "I don't think a good actor ever stops learning and honing their craft, and I want to be the best I can. So, yeah, I learned a lot working in TV, but my heart will always be in theater."

She nods and waves to a group of the actors who signal they're leaving for home after everybody worked to stow the props.

Tommy turns to follow them, calling over his shoulder, "See you tomorrow."

I walk with Asia to the lighting booth to retrieve our jackets and my backpack.

"The actors from your community theater group are much better than I expected," she says.

"I think it's a pretty cohesive troupe because we used to run plays year-round, giving them plenty of experience. They also have the dynamite script you've written. I could never make it as a playwright, but you're amazing. A great script makes the acting better and a lot more fun."

Her neck and cheeks flush pink, but I pretend not to notice. I want her to take the compliment as genuine praise, not flirting. "Thanks. It's what I want to do—write, direct, and produce. I've never wanted to be onstage like you are."

"Yeah, well, acting is about all I'm good at, so it's on the stage or in front of the cameras for me. It's not actually an ego thing."

She laughs. "Yes, it is."

I smile. "Okay. Maybe some of what drives me is ego."

We retrieve our things, shut everything down, and lock up as we exit the building. Then we pause outside.

"You need a lift?" I point to my Jeep nearby on the street. "I'm parked right over there."

"Thanks, but I have my bike, and it's equipped with lights. I rent a garage apartment less than a mile from here, and it's neighborhood streets all the way."

I see a bicycle chained to a tree on the side of the building and nod. "Yeah. Christmas is pretty bike and pedestrian friendly. We don't have much crime around here either." That is true in the central part of town, the area permanently decorated for the holidays. The strip malls, rowdy bars, chain restaurants, and car dealerships are on the highway at the outskirts of town.

We both hesitate for an awkward moment.

"Asia?"

Her expression is instantly guarded, and I realize she's expecting me to flirt.

"Thanks for letting me do this. I can't remember when I've enjoyed something so much."

She blinks at me, and then her eyes soften. "You are good at something other than acting."

"Flirting?" I take a step back and throw my hands up in mock horror. "I'm not flirting with you, I promise."

She shakes her head but smiles. "No, you nutcase. Acting might come naturally to you, but you're a good teacher, too."

I warm at her name-calling because it holds a hint of affection, and I grab onto that to savor later. "Nah. I just show them what I'd do."

She waves me off as she walks backward a few steps to her bicycle. "Whatever. Tomorrow. I'll be here at noon." She's starting and ending some of the rehearsals later to accommodate the locals who have regular jobs during the day.

I wave back. "I have to take Mom to a doctor's appointment at two, but I'll be here after that."

"See you then," she says.

I wait while she unchains her bike and adjusts her messenger bag across her shoulders, then give a final wave as she pedals out of sight. Something about that woman draws me, even though a little voice in my head is screaming that I'm going to get burned. Again.

❖

"It's been three weeks, Phil, and all you've come up with is that cattle call for a bit part?"

"This ain't Hollywood, kid, with a hundred opportunities out there. Some off-Broadway touring roles are coming up."

"I'm totally on board with that," I say. I've heard those traveling troupes can be one long party between cities and performances. "Just keep looking for me, Phil. I need the work."

"I do have some news that might interest you." It sounds like he's puffing a cigar while he talks to me on the phone. He's such a stereotype. Gotta love him.

"What's that?" What could possibly interest me more than a job?

"I take it you know who Joel Lowenstein is."

"The theater critic. Who doesn't know Joel Lowenstein?" I hear myself picking up the New York mobster cadence of his speech and shake my head to get it out of my brain.

"His mother lives in your town."

"Here in Christmas?" Could Mom's friend, Mrs. Lowenstein, be Joel's mother?

"Yep. She's getting up in age and doesn't want to come to New York for Thanksgiving, then again for Hanukkah like she usually does, so he's going to spend Thanksgiving with her there and bring her here for the week of Hanukkah."

I mull over this information. "When's Hanukkah? Don't judge. What I know about religious holidays is limited to those that involve gifts from Santa or the Easter bunny."

"It moves around according to the Jewish calendar and lasts eight days."

"Yeah, yeah. I do know that much." Tommy's Jewish, and we've been friends forever. "When is it this year?"

"Starts at sundown Christmas Day and runs through the second of January."

Hmm. So he'll probably be here for several weeks before he takes her back to New York with him. "What are the chances we could get him to come see our show?"

"Next to none, I'd say, but you never know unless you try. If you're good enough on that stage, a word of endorsement from him would be a game-changer in landing a decent supporting role."

I don't answer right away because my mind is stumbling over the fact that I won't be onstage. I'm not part of the cast.

"You still there, kid?"

"Yeah. Just thinking. Thanks for the info. I'll look into it."

❖

"Guess who's coming to dinner?"

Asia eyes me with suspicion. "I'm afraid to ask."

"You." I prop one shoulder against the lighting-booth console, cross my legs at the ankles, and give her the cocky grin she once hated. Our interactions are much friendlier and more relaxed after working together for weeks, so she pinches my cheek.

"You're cute, but I still won't go out with you," she says.

"You will when you hear my news."

She turns away and starts shuffling script notes. We're only a couple of weeks away from our opening night the Saturday after Thanksgiving. "What news is that?"

"Joel Lowenstein is going to be in town for a couple of weeks, visiting his mother for Thanksgiving."

She freezes her paper-shuffling and turns back slowly to me. "*The* Joel Lowenstein?"

"The one and only."

"You're going to have dinner with him?"

I shake my head but keep smiling. "No. I'm inviting you to dinner at my house."

She narrows her eyes. "Where will your mother be?"

"Oh, she'll be there, too. I want her to meet you."

"Why do you want your mother to meet me?"

"Well, she already likes me, but I want her to like you, too, so she'll convince her friend, Mrs. Lowenstein, to bring her son, Joel, to see our show while he's here." Whew. That was a lot to say.

Her eyes widen, and her jaw drops so that her mouth forms a nearly perfect *O*. "Your mother is friends with Joel Lowenstein's mother?" I'd nearly wet my pants when Mom confirmed this fact earlier.

"They've played bridge in the same foursome every Tuesday night for years."

In the next second, she launches herself at me, jumping into my arms and wrapping her arms and legs around me. "I could kiss you!"

I consider that remark permission and give her a brief smack on the lips. We both freeze, our faces inches away, our breath mingling. I prepare myself for her to loosen her hold and step back. Instead, she tightens her slender body around me and touches her lips to mine again, tentatively at first, then more firmly. I let her take the lead and open readily when I feel her tongue against my lips. She's soft and warm and tastes like the peppermint tea she likes to drink.

A door slams somewhere in the theater, and we stare at each other as we pull back. Her hazel eyes, which change with her moods, are almost green.

"We should keep this between us for now," she says, releasing me and stepping back even more.

Our kiss or the critic? She apparently reads the question in my eyes and clarifies her remark.

"The news about Joel. It might not happen, and if it does, knowing he's in the audience might make the cast too nervous."

I nod, but that isn't the question I want her to answer. "Can we talk about that kiss later?"

"No." She reaches up to touch my lips with her fingers. "Maybe."

"Okay." I'm not going to push. The cocky confidence I normally project is all bravado. I've never seriously pursued a woman. Lisa Langston made the first move on me. And before I took off for California, Susan had flirted shamelessly with me for months before I crawled into bed with her. This uncertain dance with Asia is new ground for me.

CHAPTER TEN

My mouth waters when I lift the lid and sniff the stroganoff Mr. Healy has made for our dinner. Mom suggested that we invite him to help move the conversation along. He's a talker and at ease with almost anyone, so I agreed.

"We really didn't invite you so you'd cook, Mr. Healy, but Mom and I appreciate it."

"Please. It's Al. You're not a kid anymore, so let's speak to each other as adults," he says. "It's my pleasure to cook for you ladies." He fusses with the place settings on the breakfast table. It seats four in a more informal yet intimate way, and the dining-room table is currently covered with a jigsaw puzzle. "I'll wait until your guest arrives to put on the pasta and broccoli. Both tend to get mushy if heated too long."

I glance at my watch. "I better go pick her up now." Typical of many New Yorkers, Asia relies on public transportation, but Christmas has only a few buses that run between the strip malls' large parking lots and the downtown area, which has limited parking. Her bicycle is fine for getting from her apartment to downtown, but Mom's house is a bit far for a bike ride at night. The doorbell rings as I grab my keys from their hook. To my surprise, it's Asia.

"Hey. I was about to come pick you up."

"Tommy was at the theater, too, so he offered to drop me off on his way home." She turns and waves good-bye as he's backing out of the driveway.

I frown but step back to let her come inside. "I was going to pick you up," I say again.

She slaps me across the stomach as she walks past me. "Chill. It's not like this is a date or anything."

Maybe I want it to be a date. I follow her to take her coat just as Mom emerges from the bedroom to join Al, and then I make the introductions.

"You didn't tell us how pretty she is," Al says, taking her hand in both of his large ones.

I shrug, still sulking over not getting to pick her up.

"Davis and Asia are working together at the community theater." Mom jumps in to distract Al before he says too much to imply this is a date…because he and Mom both know I was thinking of it as one. "She has a fellowship to produce this year's holiday play."

Malleable as always, Al is easy to redirect. "Wonderful. We want to hear all about the show tonight." He goes over to the stove. "I was waiting because I thought Davis was going to go get you, but I'll start the pasta and broccoli now."

"Come and sit down," Mom says to Asia, walking over to the facing sofas in the living-room area. She had some walls knocked down years ago to convert the area to an open concept. "Davis, would you pour us some wine? Just a little for me because I'm still on an antibiotic."

I obediently open the French Syrah I've carefully chosen to pair with Al's stroganoff and pour four glasses.

"So, Asia. Davis tells me that you're not only producing and directing this show, but that you've written an original script for it." Having spent years drawing information out of third-graders, Mom is adept at getting people to talk about themselves.

Asia accepts the wineglass I offer her. "Well, I was fortunate enough to be accepted for a new fellowship that provides limited funding to aspiring playwrights if they produce their play in conjunction with a community theater. The Christmas Community Theater was a perfect choice because of its strong history of successful shows and solid base of experienced amateur actors."

Mom nods. "I was taking Bryan and Davis to the shows every Christmas when Davis was still a toddler. We were amazed that she would sit so still at that age, mesmerized by the actors. She was only eight years old when she got her first speaking part on that very stage." She smiles at me.

I sit on the sofa next to Asia, not too close but not too far, so Al can sit next to Mom once he gets things going in the kitchen. Asia smiles at me. "I bet she was adorable. What part was she playing?"

Mom's warming to her subject. "It was a musical. Davis is with five other children, who persuade her to sneak downstairs where she sees their mother kissing Santa Claus. She rushes back to the other children, and they sing a modified version of 'I Saw Mama Kissing Santa Claus.'"

My neck and ears are heating, and Asia's smile is growing. "I didn't know you sing, too," she says.

"I think the album with photos of her in that play is in the spare room. Go get it, Davis."

"No, Mom. Dinner's going to be ready in a few minutes. You have stacks of stuff in there. I'll never find it."

Undeterred, Mom turns back to Asia. "She was so cute. She even got a mention when the local paper reviewed the show. She just had a few lines. Do them for Asia and Al, honey."

"Mom." I draw out her name in supplication. I'm trying to impress Asia, not look stupid.

Asia presses her hands together in a begging gesture. "Please. I'd love to see your part."

"I'm not a kid anymore, so it won't be cute like it was then."

Asia raises an elegant eyebrow over one beautiful eye. "Are you saying it's beyond your acting capabilities?"

I can withstand begging, but I'm incapable of walking away from a challenge. I stand, chin held high in as dignified a pose as possible, and walk to the right for several steps before charging back to crouch in front of the fireplace and exclaim, "I saw Mama kissing Santa Claus!" Then I look to the left and stage-whisper to imaginary children, "I did, too." Then I launch into the song, giving them the full performance. When I finish, everyone's clapping, while Mom and Asia are laughing so hard they're both wiping away tears.

Al helps my mom rise from the sofa. "And now for the second act, dinner is served," he says.

The meal is delicious and the conversation wonderful. Mom and Al talk about their cooking class, I tell some stories about previous shows at the theater, and Asia offers a little about her childhood. Her parents were medical missionaries who spent most of their careers in remote and often rustic areas around the world, so once she was old enough to go to school, she begged and was allowed to live with her aunt, a professor in London. Her aunt loved theater and often took Asia to see shows. She avoids saying anything more about her parents but speaks fondly of her aunt.

Asia begins to help Al clear the dishes to serve coffee and dessert, so I nod to let her know I'm going to introduce the secondary purpose of our dinner. Well, the subject of Joel Lowenstein *is* why Asia accepted my invitation. I mainly wanted to spend time with her.

"Mom, do you still play bridge with Mrs. Lowenstein?"

"Cora? Yes. But we aren't partners anymore since Al started playing with me."

"You shoulda stuck with her, Ida. She's a better player than me," Al says as he places a slice of Mom's favorite lemon chess pie in front of her. "I didn't mean to horn in on your partnership."

"Don't be silly," Mom says, giving him an affectionate look. "Cora's happy playing with Joyce because she's a big gossip and Cora's nosy."

"But you still see her?"

"Oh, yes. We sometimes play against her and Joyce."

Al laughs and sits to eat his dessert now that we're all served. "Because I'm nosy, too."

Mom swats at his arm. "Yes, you are."

I clear my throat to draw attention back to me. "Did you know what her son, Joel, does now?"

Mom rolls her eyes. "As if Cora doesn't constantly remind us. He writes theater reviews, doesn't he?"

"More than that, he's one of the most respected theater critics in the city."

"Really?"

"Yes. And, well, I've heard that he's coming here to celebrate Thanksgiving with Cora. If there's any way we could get him to review our show, it would be amazing."

"Oh, I don't know," Mom says. "If he's such a big deal, I doubt he'd go watch something at a community theater."

"Mrs. Hart. I mean, Ida." Asia reaches for Mom's hand. "I'm not going to pretend I don't have some self-interest in this request. A good review from him could open professional doors for me. But this is about more than my career. Mr. Fogel's nephew isn't interested in theater any longer, so he's not going to fund any more shows here. My show very well might be the last if it's not successful enough to bring the tourists back to Christmas, and the town's shops depend on the tourist trade."

Al nods his agreement. "It's true. Several shops that reopened after the pandemic couldn't stay afloat because they weren't making enough sales. I heard the Johnstons just locked the doors on their gift shop one morning and never opened back up. All the merchandise is still on the shelves, collecting dust."

I give Mom my most imploring expression. "Maybe Cora can convince Joel to take her to the show while he's here. Even a mention in his column could have a big impact."

She pulls her hand from Asia's and slaps me on the arm. "You don't have to turn that practiced puppy-dog look on me, brat," she says. "Al and I will go to bridge club next week and see what we can do."

I clap my hands together, and Asia beams. "Yes! When Mom puts her mind to something, nothing stops her."

Al is less enthusiastic. "Ida, dear. Are you sure you're well enough to go to bridge club?"

She pats his hand. "I'm about to go stir-crazy stuck here in this house. If I get too tired, I'll let you bring me home early."

He nods, looking at her intently, most likely for any obvious signs of pain, weariness, or too much of a brave front. "Okay. As long as you promise to be honest and let me know if you hurt or get too tired."

"I promise." Mom rises gingerly from her chair. "In fact, I'm a bit tired right now."

All three of us jump up, offering an arm or taking one of her hands to assist her. She bats us away, except for Al, whose arm she accepts to steady herself. "Davis, you go ahead and take Asia home." She briefly clasps Asia's forearm. "It was lovely to meet you, sweetie. I'm so looking forward to seeing your show."

❖

The air is crisp and smelling of snow too early in the season when I walk Asia out to my car to drive her home. Maybe it's just wishful thinking on my part, since I've been living snowless in California for the past five years. Still, the fluffy stuff seems like a possibility as we drive through the quiet streets of Christmas, its year-round holiday lights twinkling from old-style streetlights and storefronts. Thanksgiving is more than a week away, yet the air is already electric with the anticipation of a visit from the fat guy in the red suit.

Asia seems to be picking up on my thoughts…or I'm picking up on hers. "Do you find yourself jaded about the holidays after growing up with Santa stuff year-round?"

"Are you kidding? Nothing trumps the fun of Santa Claus, although it can be like torture at times. You barely have time to enjoy your toys from one Christmas before you're thinking about what to ask for next December. The anticipation is so drawn out, it's excruciating. Sort of like having a hard-on, but relief is nine or ten months away."

"Ewww. That's gross." She thumps me on the shoulder. "Now I'm going to have that image in my head every time I think of Christmas."

I laugh and park in front of the coffee shop, which is about to close. "I'll just be a minute." I jump out of my car and jog into the shop, which is empty of other customers at this late hour.

The barista greets me with a smile and begins topping two large hot chocolates with tall swirls of whipped cream. "Got your order ready. I was just waiting for you to get here to add the whipped cream."

"Thanks a million. You ran my card already, right?"

"Yep. You're good to go…and I deleted the text with your card number already." She hands over the two large cups. "You shouldn't put your credit-card information in a text, you know. Someone could steal your identity."

I grin. "Or my favorite barista could run it for my purchase, then delete it so nobody could steal it." I hold up the cups. "Thanks for helping me." Then I sprint out the door and back to Asia.

I hand her both cups. "Hang on to these. I want to show you something better to picture when you think of our little town."

I drive us to a small park on the north border of the downtown shopping area. Because it's late, we're completely alone. I grab my phone and one of the hot chocolates from her. "Come on. This is something you need to see." I take her hand when she gets out of the car and don't let go as I walk her down a dark path through a strip of leafless birch and fluffy fir trees.

"Are you sure this is safe?" She seems hesitant, trailing behind a little, so I tug her along.

"I know you're used to New York parks that are littered with homeless and druggies after dark, but this is Christmas. We're perfectly safe." At that moment, we emerge from the woods, where several benches sit empty on the grassy shore of a one-acre pond.

The moon is only a sliver, but the night sky's littered with thousands of stars. I guide her to a bench at the center of the clearing, and then we cup our drinks to warm our hands and sip hot chocolate to ward off the cold. The evening is quiet except for the occasional hoot of an owl prowling for a midnight snack.

She looks up at the stars. "This is beautiful."

"Wait till you see the show," I say, picking up my phone. I tap away at several screens, then pause with my finger hovering over the screen. "Ready?"

Asia looks at me, both eyebrows raised.

"Don't look at me." I point toward the pond. "Watch out there."

The first strains of "Here Comes Santa Claus" sound from my iPhone, and the birch trees lining the pond's shore come to life with white, then colored lights flashing to the beat of the music.

Asia sounds delighted as she laughs, and she looks enchanted. "It's like the trees are dancing."

Elation swells my chest. Damn. She is so beautiful. I tap my phone one more time, and Rudolph appears at one end of the pond, leading his team of reindeer that are pulling Santa in his sleigh.

"Santa!"

The entire ensemble consists of a series of lights flickering in a pattern that gives the reindeers' legs an illusion of motion. They and the sleigh roller-coaster across the pond on a mostly underwater mechanism, then disappear into the woods at the opposite end, where a turnaround is carved into that bank, hidden by a cluster of Douglas firs.

"You did that with your phone?" She turns to me, eyes shining.

"Yep. It's an automated system that normally moves Santa

across the pond twice during the song, but one of Tommy's nerd friends in high school figured out how to hack into the system and made an app he shared with some of us so we can run it on our own." I show her the app on my phone, then point to what looks like a utility box to our left. "The real controls are in that metal box over there. Want to see it again?"

She nods enthusiastically, so I hold my phone out for her to hit the start button. We watch the little Santa show three more times before our drinks are long gone and clouds have mostly obscured the stars. I take her cold hand in my warm one again for our return walk under the pretense of guiding her through the dark woods, and she doesn't pull away.

Our drive to her Airbnb studio apartment over Tommy's great-uncle's two-car garage is short and quiet. So much of the town's population is related by blood or marriage that we all know the difference between a second cousin and a cousin twice removed. I don't give her time to protest as I hop out of the car to walk her to her apartment. She gives me an odd look but allows me to follow her up the exterior steps to her door. When we reach the top, she draws her keys from her pocket and turns to me.

"Thanks for everything tonight," she says. "I enjoyed dinner. You mother and her boyfriend are really great."

"Oh. Al isn't her boyfriend. He's our neighbor."

She chuckles. "Are you blind? They are so cute together."

I frown. "They're just friends."

"Whatever." She shakes her head at my denial and leans back against the door. "The thing at the park is really...I wasn't so sure when you led me into those woods...I don't know when I've seen so many stars..." She seems to be having trouble putting a full sentence together as I edge closer and take her keys from her hand. My face is inches from hers as I fit the door key into the lock and turn it.

"Davis, I think we should talk about that kiss," she says.

I move closer, my mouth inches from her mouth, the steam of our warm breath mingling in the cold air, and I murmur against her soft, soft lips. "I don't want to talk about it. I want to relive it." I'm all in, do or die, no longer waiting for spoken permission because there is clear consent in her eyes and in her hands pulling my hips against hers. She is warm and pliant, even eager in returning my kiss. Finally, I gently disengage and gaze into eyes swirling with green and gray and flecked with sparks of gold.

"This is not a good idea." Her words are a breathless whisper.

"I don't want to hear why, because I think it's a very, very good idea." I quickly brush my lips against hers again, then turn and sprint down the stairs to my car. I leave without looking back or giving her a chance to spoil this flawless evening and another perfect kiss.

CHAPTER ELEVEN

When I soundly kissed Asia, then left her on the landing outside her door, I intended to leave her hungry for more. Ha. I'm the one left wanting. For the first time in years, I skip my nightly routine of washing my face, then applying a three-layer regimen of collagen, skin-tightener, and moisturizer. I fancy I can still feel the touch of her hand on my cheek and her lips on mine.

I'm sleeping in my own bedroom now since Mom is getting around fine with her walker. I did get a cute basket that attaches to it so she can carry her phone to call me from her bedroom if she needs help. Tonight, however, I'm tempted to settle in her recliner to sleep so I can resist the temptation to slide my fingers down my belly and into the abundant moisture caused by Asia's kiss and renewed every time I relive the moment. I have this odd desire—one that I can't even begin to fully understand—for my next orgasm to be by her hand or from her tongue.

Mom, however, is already asleep, so I decide not to risk waking her by going into her room. I normally sleep naked, but with my history of making bad decisions when I'm naked, I don't take off my boy-short underwear and pull on a pair of gym shorts for an extra barrier should my fingers stray. Just for good measure, I climb into bed but keep my hands on top of the covers because I know I'll relive that kiss in my dreams. The power Asia has over me is scary, but I wallow deliciously in it rather than seek escape. At least for now, I close my eyes and try to focus on the next step in my mission to woo her.

❖

I wake gasping for air, my heart racing and the pleasant tingle of orgasm washing through my belly. Holy crap. My hips jerk with the small waves of pleasure in the aftermath. Shit. I can't remember the specifics of my dream because I'm still trying to catch my breath. Damn. I actually climaxed in my sleep. This has never happened to me. Never.

I press a hand to my chest, trying to calm the pounding of my heart, and attempt to recall my last thoughts that could have triggered this. I was searching for a special date to impress Asia. Whew. My heart hasn't pounded like this since the first time I stepped onstage in front of an audience.

Broadway.

It comes to me, crystal clear like bright stage lights. I'll invite her to see a play with me in the city. Thanksgiving and our show's premiere are about a week away, and I know she has planned rehearsals Thanksgiving evening and Friday before the opening on Saturday. But she's giving the cast the day off the Wednesday before Thanksgiving.

This epiphany isn't helping slow my heart. I jump out of bed. Damn, the floor is cold. I pull on some thick socks and a flannel bathrobe, which I left here when I moved out West.

Mom is up and making coffee. I'm surprised to see she's getting around without her walker now.

"You should invite Asia over for Thanksgiving dinner," she says.

"I thought about ordering takeout. That Cracker Barrel out on the highway is offering a complete Thanksgiving meal, so you wouldn't have to tire yourself out half the day."

"Absolutely not. Al plans to cook the turkey and dressing at his house. We need to handle only dessert and the side dishes. You should invite any other of your theater group's holiday orphans to come, too."

"I'll ask, but I think David and Bruce have already done that."

Mom stops pouring coffee for both of us for a minute. "Do you think Asia's going to their house?"

"Not if I can help it." I smile. "I intend to ask her to go see a Broadway play on Wednesday because we're not rehearsing that day, then bring her here for Thanksgiving."

"Really? I would think you'd be rehearsing every day the week before the opening."

"Everything's going really smoothly, so she thought giving everybody a break might be helpful since she's holding rehearsal late Thursday. Students make up about half the cast, so they'll have time to drive back to New York on Wednesday, have dinner with their families or friends there early Thursday, and be back for a six o'clock rehearsal."

"That's nice of her."

"I think it's more of a psychological ploy. The kids are losing focus, whether from the holidays or nerves, and it's starting to show. A break might help." I take a box of blueberry waffles from the freezer. "Sit down, Mom. I'll cook breakfast."

She chuckles but takes her coffee and sits at the kitchen island. "I don't think reheating frozen waffles counts as cooking."

"We're going to have bacon, too."

She wrinkles her nose. "That's okay, honey. I know you're doing your best, but you don't cook. I don't like that pre-cooked bacon."

"Neither do I." I take out a plate and cover it with a paper towel. "But I do know how to cook bacon in a microwave." I lay out strips of bacon on the paper towel, then place another on top of the bacon.

"Not in a frying pan?"

"Nope." I slide the plate into the microwave and set it to four minutes. "It's a lot less messy this way. The paper towels soak up the grease, and you just throw them in the trash."

"I like my bacon crispy."

"I can make it crispy." I pop a couple of waffle squares in the toaster and pour maple syrup into a glass measuring cup to warm it. That will go in the microwave when the bacon's done. "Just try to trust me."

Mom seems to consider this request. "Okay. I'll trust you," she says.

The microwave dings, and I check the bacon. "Another two minutes," I tell her.

The toaster pops up the heated waffles, and I plop them onto a plate and brush them with melted butter. When the microwave dings again, I add bacon to the plate, then put two waffle squares in the toaster for me. Then the syrup goes into the microwave for a minute while I freshen Mom's coffee.

"I'm impressed," she says. "This is a five-star breakfast."

"Well, over the past five years I did have to feed myself occasionally." The microwave dings again, and I put the warmed syrup on the table for her while I load a plate for me. I feel Mom watching me, so I give her an inquiring look when I sit down. "What?"

"You really like her, don't you?"

"Who?" I try to be nonchalant, but the heat climbing up my neck to my ears and cheeks gives me away.

Mom actually throws her head back and laughs. "That's the worst example of acting I've ever seen from you. And it answers my question."

My ears and cheeks are burning now, so I stuff a forkful of waffle into my mouth. Mom pats my arm, her gaze full of affection.

"I won't tease you, but I want you to tell me. She's different from the other women you've liked?"

I try another ploy to get out from under her spotlight. "What's up with you and Al?"

She sits back in her chair and takes a bite of bacon. "I had no idea you could cook bacon so well in a microwave."

I see how things are. She's mocking me. "How about this? You fess up about you and Al, and then I'll tell you about Asia."

She narrows her eyes, no doubt weighing whether I'll hold up my end of the deal if she goes first, then talks as she resumes eating. "Before your father took off to parts unknown, we were friends with Al and his wife, Theresa. After your father left, they were a great support for me. Al mowed my lawn, and Theresa often helped me with you and your brother. So, when Theresa got sick and died two years ago, I tried to help Al through his grief as much as I could. We grew closer, and then one day we became more than friends. He's been courting me for almost a year." She frowned down at her plate. "I don't want to complain, but this back surgery and you living here has put a halt to our bedroom time."

I slap my hands over my ears. "La-la-la. I don't want to know about my mother doing the nasty with our neighbor."

She laughs but raises an eyebrow. "But I do want to know about your crush on Asia."

I drop my hands back to the table and grab a piece of bacon to gnaw on while I choose my words. "She hates my celebrity status, which is a switch from everybody else who just wants to sleep with me because I'm...was...an actor on a hit show. So it's taken me a while to get her to stop banning me from the theater."

"Is that what draws you to her, the fact that she's hard to get?"

Was it? I stuff my last bite of waffle into my mouth and think about the possibility before shaking my head. "No. The instant I saw her in the coffee shop, before she spoke to me and threw me out of the theater, I was drawn to her eyes and her unique beauty. But as I've gotten to know her, I've realized she's incredibly smart and driven. She knows what she wants and is going after it."

"What does she want?"

"She wants to write and produce plays...maybe direct, too."

"She's not interested in television or movies?"

"I don't think so. I know theater has limited opportunities, though, so she might end up writing some screenplays, too."

"What if she doesn't succeed at breaking into theater? Does she have a plan B?"

I shove my empty plate away. "Hell. I don't know. I haven't shared my future plans with her either, even though my plan B is simply to find acting work, any acting work." I collect our plates and silverware and take them to the sink to wash. "We haven't even slept together, much less talked about anything past our last kiss." I drop my chin to my chest. "I'm not even sure I can call this a relationship yet. She's like a spirited horse, and I'm scared she's going to bolt if she thinks I'm trying to rope her in."

Mom stands and comes over to hug me from behind. "I think that's good for you. Everything has always come too easy for you, Davis—friends, grades, your career. I'm not saying you've never worked hard. It's just that your talent and good looks have always given you an advantage. Hopefully, if this does become a relationship, you'll take time to examine your feelings toward her and how deep or shallow they run."

I heave a big sigh. "This is just so hard." I pause to hold back my thought, but this is Mom, and her very presence makes me want to bare my soul like a child. "Besides, the way my career is floundering right now, I feel a little raw. I guess 'exposed' is the word I'm searching for."

She gives me a squeeze before releasing me and going for another coffee refill. "Now tell me which show you're planning to take her to see."

CHAPTER TWELVE

The Lion King? I love that show." Asia's eyes are bright with enthusiasm.

"It's my favorite, and my agent got two tickets comped by the director, who's a friend of his."

Asia's expression grows serious. "Maybe your mom would like to go."

I shake my head. "She's not a hundred percent yet and didn't think she could handle the trip, dinner, and then the play. I can get tickets for her and Al some other time."

"Her and Al, huh?" She bumps my shoulder as we leave the lighting booth and walk down to the stage.

Damn it. My neck and ears are heating up again. "Uh, yeah. She admitted the two of them have been dating for a while." I look away because I can't meet her eyes while voicing my next confession. "Mom said her back surgery, then my living at the house, has put a crimp in their"—I lift my hands to make air quotes—"bedroom time."

Asia laughs at my expense but hooks her arm in mine. "You're embarrassed. That's so cute."

"She's always cute," Tommy says from behind before he pushes his way between us. "But she's rarely embarrassed. Tell me, tell me."

"Davis has found out her mom is sleeping with the widower next door."

Tommy dramatically throws his hand up to his mouth. "I suspected Ida had some secret slut in her."

I punch him on the arm. "That's my mother you're talking about."

Tommy gives me a one-armed hug. "Kidding. You know I love Ida, much more than my own mom."

It's true. Tommy spent endless days at my house when we were growing up, and when Tommy's mother refused to come to his wedding because he was marrying a man, Mom sat in the place reserved for the groom's mother.

He's suddenly serious, his arm still slung over my shoulder. "You okay with this? I mean, your dad took off years ago."

"Fifteen years. I was ten."

"And your mom hasn't dated anyone during the entire time?"

"Nope. Not that I know about."

Asia stares at me, eyes wide. "Never?"

I shake my head. "I don't know if she was waiting for my dad to come back or if she just didn't have time to date. She taught school and spent her free time with me and Bryan, taking me to acting classes and plays, and going to Bryan's basketball and baseball games."

We reach the stage, and Tommy gives me a little squeeze before heading to the wings to help get the set ready. Asia lingers, then wraps her hand around my forearm. "Your mom looks really happy. Maybe it's time for her to live for herself."

She's right, of course. "I know. It's just hard to think of her as anything but my mom. And I sure don't want to think about her having sex."

Asia bumps my shoulder with hers. "What kid does? But I sure as hell hope I still have a sex life at her age."

Time for a subject change. "So, you'll go with me to see *The Lion King*?"

"Yes! It's one of my favorites."

"Great. Plan to stay in the city overnight. We'll have dinner, then go see the show, and drive back Thursday morning in plenty of time to help Mom prepare Thanksgiving dinner. You are going to eat with us, aren't you?"

She hesitates, her brows pulling together as if she's thinking hard.

"You'll break Mom's heart if you don't come. She really likes you." I give her a slight bow. "Staying overnight is not a presumption of anything other than dinner and the theater." I hold up my hand, pinkie extended. "Pinkie swear."

She narrows her eyes, but her shoulders relax with that promise. "Okay." She turns to the stage and claps her hands together. "Okay, people. Let's get started. I want to focus on Act Two."

❖

I need to get some work soon because I'm blowing the last of my money on my Broadway date with Asia. Stupid, I know, but something about this woman is making me desperate to impress her. So, when an administrator from the community college at a nearby, much larger town calls and asks if I will be a guest lecturer for their media and drama programs, it looks like easy union-approved money. The offer is at the last minute, and the woman says Tommy recommended me when their original guest teacher backed out. I jump at the chance. How hard can it be?

"So, how hot is Lisa Langston in bed?"

They quit raising their hands and shout out questions like paparazzi.

"Did they kill you off the show because you outed her?"

"Do you think other closeted celebrities should be outed to give the LGBTQ community more visibility?"

I hold up my hands to quiet them. "Nondisclosure agreements are routine in acting contracts, so I cannot comment on any of that." It's a small lie. The NDA I signed was connected to a promise from the show's lawyers that they would only confiscate my pay and I wouldn't be sued for defaming their star. "After we cover some ideas for using social media to raise your profile or that of your company, I'll be happy to answer general questions about breaking into showbiz as a career."

A slender boy in the back of the class holds his hand up.

"Yes?"

"Did they know you were gay when they hired you?"

I tilt my head. This is a question I can answer. "Honestly, nobody asked, and it didn't occur to me that it had anything to do with the role I was auditioning for. There are many people in the public eye who prefer to be known for their accomplishments rather than their sexual orientation. For example, Sally Ride. She was a scientist and an astronaut. She had a longtime partner. Her family, friends, and colleagues knew, but she never officially announced that she was a lesbian because her sexual orientation had nothing to do with her accomplishments. She simply wanted to be an example for all little girls aspiring to a career in the science field."

The expressions on the faces of several students tell me they don't agree with her keeping her private life private. So, I elaborate.

"I think many actors are afraid of being typecast according to gay and lesbian stereotypes, the same way a successful comedic actor might be overlooked for a dramatic role. Child actors often find it hard to transition to adult roles because casting directors feel the public still sees them as children, rather than as adult characters. A professional actor should be able to play many roles, sort of like an impressionist can transform their voice and mannerisms to mimic someone else."

"Can you do that?" The question comes from the back of the amphitheater-style lecture hall, but I recognize Asia's voice.

I grin. "Give me a few lines, and I'll show you." The improv group I used to hang out with in college routinely ran through this exercise for fun and to loosen up.

"Where have you been?" A male student supplies my line.

I widen my stance, square my shoulders, and pace back

and forth in an aggressive manner. "Where have you been?" My voice comes out deeper and the words a hard staccato.

Then I pull in my stance, soften my shoulders, and run my fingers through my hair in a gesture of frustration before bending at the waist with my hands on my hips as though leaning over a child. "Where have you been?"

Finally, I bend my knees and waist, and hunch my shoulders to make my body appear smaller. I mimic rubbing tears away from my eyes with my fists and change my voice to a tearful child's. "Where have you been?"

My display draws applause from most of the students, except the ones afraid to look uncool.

"Thank you. That leads us to the subject of this lecture. Acting is really illusion, just like the magician who appears to produce a card or coin out of thin air. Subliminal illusion is a tool advertisers use to sell their products. You're looking online for new car insurance, and you recognize the name of that company represented by the gecko with an Australian accent. Your brain says, 'We like that little fellow,' so you decide to get a quote from that company."

I'm soon lost in my subject matter and interaction with the students, forgetting about Asia, who finds a seat in the uppermost row, until another instructor waves at me from the side of the podium to let me know it's time for his class to begin.

"Looks like our time is up. Thanks. You guys were great. Maybe I'll see you again after your winter break."

I sprint up the tiers of seats to Asia, mostly so no students can stop me to talk or ask for an autograph. I don't mind giving autographs, just not today when the woman who is haunting my dreams each night is waiting.

"Hey. I'm surprised to see you here."

She pushes thick curls back away from her face. "I'm subbing a couple of days for a friend who teaches a writing class here. Tommy told me you were doing a few guest lectures here, too, so I decided to check you out."

"Huh. I've been checking you out for months," I say, and we smile at each other. I want to take her hand in mine, but I'm unsure how she feels about public displays of affection. "How did you get here?" I know she doesn't have a car.

"I drove my friend to the airport, and she left her car with me so I could get back and forth to campus."

I squint at her in mock scrutiny. "Do you even have a driver's license?" It's not a ridiculous question. Some New York City natives never learn to drive or get a license because of the ample public transportation.

She bumps my shoulder, then takes my hand in hers. "Yes. I have a driver's license. I went to school in the city but haven't always lived there."

This conversation should lead me to realize I know very little about her past or her family situation. But, at the moment, all my brain can register is her hand clasping mine. She's holding my hand in public. SHE'S HOLDING MY HAND.

"Where are you parked?"

"Her car has a sticker that lets me in faculty parking." She points to a parking lot on the other side of the grassy quad we're crossing. "Where are you parked?"

I make an unpleasant face. "On the other side of campus in one of the very few visitor lots." I suddenly develop a pronounced limp and look forlornly into the distance. "It's at least a couple of miles, and I have a terrible hangnail on my big toe."

She laughs at my antics. "I don't suppose you'd like a ride to your car?"

I slap my forehead dramatically. "Thank God. I was afraid I'd have to ask some cute co-ed for one."

"You are such an idiot." She releases my hand to backhand me across the stomach, but I recapture it, and she doesn't pull away or comment on the fact that my limp has been miraculously healed.

We climb into her friend's car, but she doesn't start the

engine right away. "You're really good at teaching," she says. "Did you know you would be?"

Her compliment heats my cheeks. "Thanks. I didn't, but I know I like coaching the actors in your play. Teaching is a lot like coaching."

She starts the car but is quiet as I direct her through campus to my vehicle. Finally, she speaks. "You did a good job deflecting those personal questions."

I stare down at my lap, unable to meet her gaze. "The whole Lisa thing wasn't my finest moment. If I could have a do-over, I'd handle it a lot more maturely."

Her voice is soft. "Can you tell me what really happened?"

I pick at a thread where my jeans are fashionably ripped. "Only if you absolutely promise never to tell anyone else. I wasn't lying when I said I had to sign a nondisclosure contract."

"I understand, and I would never mention it to anyone. But you don't have to tell me if you aren't comfortable doing it."

I shake my head, still avoiding her gaze. "It's embarrassing, but I need to confide in someone, and I can't really afford a therapist right now."

She waits patiently while I worry that thread and a few others.

"We'd been sleeping together on the down-low for a couple of months. I've never hidden my sexual orientation, but nobody has ever asked me about it. Lisa, on the other hand, is intensely closeted. I knew that, but my ego was so inflated with dating her, I just chose to ignore it. I told myself that I'd be different. I had visions of her coming out and us marrying, which just shows how immature and oblivious I was being."

Asia slides her hand into my lap to clasp mine. Her fingers are warm as they wrap around mine, while I recount the worst night and morning-after of my life.

"That was the infamous video that Lisa's marketing team discredited?"

"Yeah. Well, the jerk also had videoed Lisa and Charleigh in a heavy make-out session while at the party." I rub my face with both hands and finally look at her. "Her PR team said the make-out session was just to prank someone else at the party, or something like that. Then they painted me as a pathetic stalker who had a crush on my costar and made up a bunch of stuff about her when she rejected my advances."

"Why didn't you defend yourself? Surely some legitimate journalists would publish your side of the story."

"They said if I tried to collect the rest of my contracted pay, they'd sue me for breach of my NDA, damaging the show's image, and defaming the show's star. I didn't have the money to fight them."

"That sucks."

"Yeah." I stare down at my lap again, shame heating my face. "Besides, who was going to believe me over Lisa?"

Asia cups my chin and forces me to look at her, then plants a sweet, soft kiss on my lips. "I believe you."

"Thanks." I try to smile, but I'm sinking deep into self-pity. "So, she pretty much ruined my career on the West Coast. That's really why I'm here. I'm hoping theater people in New York won't care about what happened on the other side of the continent and will hire me for at least a minor role. My roots are in theater, so I guess that's why I want a fresh start there."

She gives my thigh a reassuring squeeze. "We're going to be late for rehearsal."

I glance at my Apple watch, glad for a way out of this heavy conversation. "Damn. You're right." I climb out of her car and use my fob to unlock my Jeep. "See you there."

Chapter Thirteen

The Marriott's manager looks up from my reservation the desk clerk has asked him to review. "Ms. Hart, this reservation for adjoining rooms is for the two of you?"

I instantly sense trouble. "Yes. I called when I made the reservation to ensure they would be adjoining."

"That's not a problem, but I have an offer you might want to consider."

I immediately shake my head. "They must be adjoining."

"Anything wrong, Davis?" Asia walks over from where she's been standing with our luggage.

"Not at all, miss," the manager says. "We've had a last-minute request from one of our frequent clients for adjoining rooms for their children, so I'd like to offer you an alternative arrangement."

I shake my head again. "Two rooms, adjoining. That's what I reserved."

Asia hooks her arm in mine. "What are you offering?"

The manager looks relieved. "I can upgrade one of your rooms to a lovely king suite at no additional cost and comp your second room. The second room, I'm afraid, is standard and one floor below the king suite."

Asia doesn't hesitate. "We'll take it."

"Asia, no. I want tonight to be perfect. I'm not staying a floor above you."

She looks at me like I'm an oblivious child, then grabs my cheeks in her hand and squeezes to kiss my fish-lips. "I know. You're taking the room one floor below me because I'm taking the suite." She accepts the key the manager hands her.

He's clearly trying not to smile as he hands over my key to the standard room a floor below her suite. "Thank you, Ms. Hart. Your concession is greatly appreciated."

I wave off the bellhop since we have only the equivalent of carry-on luggage and trail Asia to the elevators.

Once the doors close and we're zooming toward my floor, she pins me against the wall and kisses me soundly. "Stop grumbling, or you won't get lucky later in my lovely king suite."

❖

I brush an imagined speck of lint from my black tailored suit—not a tux, but close—and knock on Asia's door. I must have tried on fifty different outfits before I settled on what to bring to wear tonight. I wanted to look regal, not roguish. I straighten the collar of my gray silk shirt one more time, then adjust my gold necklace with a filigree heart pendant. At that moment, she opens the door.

"Wow." This new Asia standing before me in a form-fitting emerald dress and stylish black ankle boots with a sensible two-inch heel stuns me. Delectable, she's pulled her frizzy curls into an updo that shows off her slender neck and kissable shoulders. "You…you are gorgeous. I mean, you're always beautiful, but… wow." Not very articulate for the smooth player I've always thought myself to be. She looks me over, her eyes taking on the brilliant green of her dress.

"You clean up pretty well yourself," she says.

I give a little bow and sweep my arm toward the elevator. "May I escort you to the theater, my lady?" My feigned British accent needs more practice.

"Not with that accent I ken as English, which runs my Scottish blood hot."

I raise my eyebrows at her in mock surprise. "Descended from Jacobites?" I'm hoping she's also a fan of the streaming series *Outlander* and will get the reference.

She gives a firm nod as we head across the lobby. "On my dear mother's side."

I switch accents. "Oh, now that warms my wee Irish heart." I give her a wink. "On my father's side."

She laughs. "So that's where you get your devilish ways."

I step ahead to open the door for her. "Aye. My mum claims there's a bit of mischievous leprechaun in me. A bit of fey or no, it's hard to be good around a grand lass like you."

This is going to be a fun night.

❖

An unseasonable chill has descended with nightfall, so we pause while I help her into her coat, then tug mine on. The crisp air, our overcoats, and scarves add a bit of flair to our New York City theater adventure as we walk from the Marriott to the Minskoff Theatre for the seven o'clock showing of *The Lion King*. I take her hand to keep it warm as we stroll.

"I was thinking—"

"Oh, now that could be dangerous," she says.

I smirk at her clichéd response, then continue. "I've told you everything about me, but I don't know anything about you."

"What do you need to know?" She gives me a wary look.

"I don't *need* to know anything, but I *want* to know more about you."

"Like what?"

"Do you have brothers and sisters? Where do your parents live? Have you ever wanted to act, or do you prefer to just work behind the scenes? Have you had many girlfriends? Do you consider yourself lesbian or bisexual, or do you avoid labels altogether?"

She eyes me. "That's a lot of questions."

"Start with your family."

"I think I told you that my parents were medical missionaries, and I was basically raised by my aunt, whom I adore. I have a brother much younger than me. He apparently didn't mind living in third-world countries and being homeschooled, so he stayed with my parents. My dad, who was French, died from some jungle disease a few years ago, so my mother went home to Scotland to help run a small inn that has been passed down through her family. My brother still lives with her."

"Do you keep in touch?"

"Not much. I went to live with my aunt when I was six. Both my mother and brother feel like strangers to me." She points ahead, where the theater marquee is now visible. "I do stay in close touch with my aunt. She teaches at University College London, but we always spent our summers in Scotland, and I usually go back to visit while she's at her Scotland residence. I see my mother and brother at least once when I visit, even though I stay with my aunt."

I nod. "I was crap at keeping in touch with Mom and my brother while I was in California. The only friend I kept and spoke with frequently was Kylie, and that's because she was my agent."

"Was your agent?"

I shrug, ashamed to tell her I was a shit and fired Kylie. "She's West Coast, so I've switched to a guy on this coast with better theater connections." It's a small lie. "I'm glad I got to reconnect with Tommy because we've been friends since we were kids. No matter where my career might take me in the future, I'm not going to lose touch with him again." We walk in silence for a bit because I'm thinking of what a bad friend I am—firing Kylie and not keeping in touch with Tommy after I left for LA. I shake off my guilt. "Girlfriends? Boyfriends?"

She shrugs. "A couple of brief girlfriend relationships. Nothing significant. No boyfriends. I knew early that I was only interested in girls."

We arrive at the theater, but the line is long because the doors are still closed. I want to know more about her childhood, partly because I love the faint Scottish brogue that creeps into her speech when she talks about Scotland, but the theater opens too soon.

She turns to me, eyes alight with anticipation. "We're going in. I can't wait. Have I mentioned that *The Lion King* is my favorite show?"

I grin at her enthusiasm. "I've always loved the costumes and the music, and, and...everything about it."

We're both practically trembling with excitement when we take our seats. Theater is more than entertainment to us. It is our soul.

❖

We leave the theater arm in arm and sing the chorus of "Circle of Life" at the top of our lungs, unmindful of the other theater patrons on the sidewalk around us. Then we pause as a guy with a beautiful baritone voice starts us over with the Zulu intro to the song, and we sing the English portion again with him. Asia's voice is beautiful and blends perfectly with my passable alto. At the end of our song, we high-five the guy and decide to walk to our dinner reservation at Tony's Di Napoli several blocks away because the night chill is refreshing, and the sky is clear.

After being seated at our table and ordering, Asia squirms in her seat like she's holding back something she wants to say or ask.

"What?" I keep my inquiry soft so it doesn't sound defensive.

"Has your mother talked to Joel Lowenstein's mother yet?"

"They canceled their bridge-club meeting this week

because a lot of people were busy or going out of town for the Thanksgiving holiday."

"But I thought he was in town only for Thanksgiving. If he doesn't get here until Christmas week, it'll be too late to boost our early December ticket sales."

I reach across the table and cover her hand with mine. "Relax. My source said he's coming for Thanksgiving but staying for at least another week in exchange for his mother agreeing to go back to New York with him for the Christmas and New Year's holidays."

She stares at me pensively. "Thank you for helping me with this situation. When we first met, I thought you were completely self-involved, like most of those Hollywood types. But you don't have anything to gain if Lowenstein does review the play, do you? Our show won't do a thing to help you get an acting role here in the city."

I swallow down the fear that my acting career is dying a quick and silent death. "I already have my reward. I'd be going crazy sitting around Mom's house if I didn't have your play to go to every day. And I wouldn't have met you."

She actually rolls her eyes. "Very smooth."

I shake my head and give her my most serious look. "I wasn't trying to be."

Our waiter who's bringing our first course—bread and two different soups we opted for over salad because of the night's chill—interrupts us.

After he leaves, we taste our own soup, then taste each other's, each sipping from the other's spoon. Our sharing is decidedly intimate. And the rest of the meal goes the same, each of us holding out a forkful for the other to sample. Even when we decide to share a dessert, we continue to feed one other.

After we leave the restaurant and begin our four-block stroll back to the hotel, tiny white flakes begin to fall. Elated, we turn to each other, then lift our faces to the sky. The concrete beneath our feet and surrounding us, of course, is too warm for any of the snow to accumulate, but the air is thick with the freak flurry swirling around us. We laugh and run hand in hand the final block to our hotel.

"It's still early. Come up to my room?" she asks. "I have a complimentary bottle of wine that was included with the upgrade."

I'm mesmerized by the gray, blue, green, and flecks of gold churning in her hazel eyes but still have the presence of mind to nod and follow her to the elevators.

The suite is amazing. Much better than my standard, two-queens room...probably the only one they have in this entire fancy hotel. We open the wine and settle onto the couch to cuddle and watch the delicate snowflakes outside the floor-to-ceiling window dance downward to their demise on the city's concrete. I'm happy to let the scene inside the suite unfold at her pace. Well, not happy, but afraid to scare her off if she thinks I'm pushing because all I want to do is bed her. I put aside the nagging question of why she matters to me when so many other women haven't.

After a short while, she takes my wineglass and places it and hers on the coffee table, then turns to me. "Thank you. I've had a wonderful, magical evening."

Am I being dismissed? I'm frantically trying to conjure a delaying tactic when she takes my face in both hands and kisses me. Her touch is delicate at first, then insistent when I open to her probing tongue. I go willingly when she pulls me down to the sofa on top of her, and we kiss until we're both breathless.

She whispers while looking into my eyes, "Bedroom."

Her soft command is the only permission I need. I pull her up, then sweep her into my arms to carry her into the room where the covers are already turned back on a king-sized bed. I grab the chocolate left on the pillow, quickly unwrap it, and bathe it with my tongue while she watches, then pop it into my mouth and kiss her. As her tongue mines my mouth for the sweet treat, I reach around her to find the zipper on her dress and slide it slowly down. My hands find warm, smooth skin because she's not wearing a bra. Her only undergarment is a pair of black, lacy panties, and I nearly drool.

She works fast to divest me of my jacket, then releases the buttons of my shirt. I'm not wearing a bra either, and her hands are warm on my breasts, her thumbs electric on my rock-hard nipples.

I lock my gaze with hers and guide her onto the bed. I shed my shoes, pants, and underwear without breaking eye contact, then give her a chance to look me over before I remove her panties and cover her with my body. We both moan at the full skin contact.

Her scent is buttery as I lick her neck, then find her mouth again. She lets her hands wander down my back, then grips my buttocks. I'm so turned on that my hips buck against hers. She wraps her legs around me, and we fit together perfectly. Her sex coats mine as she urges me against her over and over, her heels digging into the back of my thighs. Damn. This is going to be quick. Too quick. I rub my sex wildly against hers as my orgasm rises, then explodes in my belly. She cries out a millisecond behind me, and I ride out our waves of pleasure as long as I can before collapsing on her, sweating and gasping for breath.

After weeks of buildup, I want more. I raise myself up to lavish attention on her small breasts, then slide down her body and shoulder between her legs.

"I don't know if I can so soon," she says.

"No rush," I say, and then I go to work. She's salty and still so hard that at first I'm careful to avoid direct contact. Her fingers are tangled in my hair, urging more, but I want to make this time last. I bathe her sex with my tongue, then probe inside as far as possible. She's tugging almost painfully at my hair, so I move up to suck her hard clit and milk her to orgasm. Her breath hitches when I plunge my fingers inside, and she bows upward as she climaxes a second later. Even then, I continue to pump into her, massaging that rough spot to bring her to a third, albeit weaker, climax.

She claws my shoulders. "No more. I can't."

I kiss each of her thighs, then crawl up to capture her lips. She's limp and sweaty and beautiful. I gather her in my arms.

"Just give me a minute." She manages to gasp out the words.

"Sleep. I've got you," I say, stroking her face, then her back.

❖

I wake to semidarkness. We didn't draw the curtains, and the glow of the never-sleeping city has replaced the brief flurry of snow outside the fully glass wall. A tingle rolls through my belly, and I suddenly realize it isn't the lights from the city that have awakened me. While sleeping I've rolled onto my side, and Asia is now at my back. Her breath is hot on my neck, and her fingers are exploring the renewed slickness between my legs.

I groan at the pleasurable pressure as she enters me from behind with her thumb and glides her fingers along my swelling clit. I move my hips to encourage her to thrust faster, harder, because my orgasm is building past the point of delay. "Oh, God. Don't stop. Don't stop." Every nerve in my body is vibrating, bursting, then trembling and jerking with the aftershocks.

She tugs me onto my back and is between my legs before I can protest. Payback. With her tongue, she expertly teases, tastes, and laps at my most sensitive tissue. She thrusts her fingers inside me, one, then two—much longer, much fuller than her thumb. She sucks my clit and I'm soaring.

❖

Much later, the sun is warm on my face, even though the glass wall has automatically darkened to control any glare. I feel the warmth at my back where she's snoring lightly, adorably against my shoulder, her arm slung around my waist to anchor herself against me. I turn slowly, hoping I won't disturb her. I want to watch her sleep. I've never wanted to watch anyone sleep before, but I crave to gaze at her without making her self-conscious. She stirs anyway, long lashes touching her cheeks as her sleepy eyes blink open.

"Hey." I keep my voice soft. "I didn't mean to wake you."

"What time is it?" She yawns and stretches catlike. "We have to get back to help your mom prepare Thanksgiving dinner."

"I was afraid you were going to back out."

She appears surprised. "I promised Ida." She sits up and looks around the room. "We need to shower and get on the road."

I stroke my hand down her smooth back. "It's early. We have plenty of time. We should luxuriate in this warm, cozy bed." I draw the words out in my sexiest voice, but she's suddenly immune to my charm and crawls to the edge of the bed. I love that she's completely at ease with her nakedness.

"Ooh. Let's order room service," she says.

She might be immune to my charm, but not to hunger. "Good idea. What do you want?"

She smacks her lips together as she thinks. I hope it's me she craves. "Belgian waffles with fruit, whipped cream, and syrup. Orange juice and coffee."

"How about I order some bacon and eggs, too, to share?"

"Fine with me. I'm starving," she says.

I pick up the phone and order while she sorts through a small suitcase for clean clothes. "Thirty minutes," I say after hanging up.

She saunters across the room, giving me a good look at her delectable behind before crooking her finger for me to come, too. "I doubt it'll take you that long," she says.

I scramble to follow her. Oh, goody. I must be the appetizer.

CHAPTER FOURTEEN

And then there was the time I got called to the school office because Davis had poked little Ronnie Smith in the eye with a cardboard sword, and he had to go to the emergency room."

Mom and Asia laugh as they chop vegetables.

I'm crying. "Why do I always have to chop the onion?" I will absolutely refuse if they ask me to cut up little red peppers.

They laugh harder at my sulk as Mom continues. "Seems Davis had them acting out a pirate story they'd read for class. I almost had to spank her to get her to apologize."

"It wasn't my fault he was a lousy swordsman." I stupidly wipe at my eye with the back of my hand as tears stream down my cheeks. "Shit." I drop my knife. Asia is by my side in an instant.

"Don't cry, Davis. I'm sure little Ronnie Smith has at least one perfectly good eye." While she's teasing me, she's also leading me over to the sink, where she squirts soap on my hands and sticks them under the water she's turned on.

"Very funny." I can't see her now because I'm squeezing my eyes shut against the burning.

"Wash your hands well," she says. I hear her opening the refrigerator.

Mom apparently knows what she's after. "Look for the little plastic lemon on the door," she says.

Then Asia is back at my side, using her hands to make sure mine are rinsed well before dousing them in lemon juice. "This will help get rid of the onion oils on your skin." She dries my hands with a towel since I'm still sightless, then turns me so that my side is against the sink. "Lean sideways so I can rinse out your eyes."

The position is awkward, and I hold on to her to keep my balance while she pours bottled water over and into my eyes. The cold refrigerated water feels good as it washes away the burn.

"Thanks," I say when the bottle's empty and she helps me stand, but I don't let go immediately. "You saved my life."

She playfully slaps my stomach with the back of her hand. "You're so dramatic."

"That's why you like me." I smile at her, aware that I must be a sight with bloodshot eyes and a runny nose triggered by my tears.

Her laughter is light. "That must be it." Then she surprises me by planting a quick kiss on my lips…right in front of my mother.

Mom chuckles. "Don't encourage her, Asia. We have enough drama around here."

There's a knock at the back door.

"I'll get it," Asia said, patting Mom's arm. "No need for you to get up."

"I can answer the door," I say, hoping this new chore might get me out of further kitchen duty.

But Asia is a few steps ahead of me. "Are you kidding? One look at those red eyes and whoever's at the door will run away." She opens the door to a grinning Al, who's holding a huge roasting pan covered in tin foil.

"Turkey's ready. Who's hungry?" He looks past Asia to smile at Mom. Then he strides into the kitchen and places the bird in one of the two ovens to keep it warm. Mom's house was built in the fifties, when most women were housewives and double ovens were popular. "I've got a few more dishes to bring over if someone wants to help me."

"I will." Asia is quick to volunteer. "Davis is still recovering from the drama, er, trauma of an onion catastrophe."

Al turns my way and shakes his head. "I was wondering about those red eyes." He pats me on the shoulder. "Happens to everybody at least once." Then he leaves with my girl in tow.

"She likes you," Mom says.

I turn to her, uncertain. "Why do you think that?"

"She might have teased you, but she was leading you over to the sink before I had time to realize what you'd done."

I can't look at Mom as my ears heat. "I hope you're right. I like her, too. A lot." I finally meet her gaze. "More than any woman I've ever dated."

Mom tilts her head. "More than that Lisa Langston woman?" I want to laugh. My mom's from the Deep South, and her use of "that woman" is clear Southern disdain. Still, I take a moment to consider what she's asking.

"I was infatuated with Lisa and caught up in the whole Hollywood scene." I shake my head. "Now that I look back, I was partly just enamored with the prestige of sleeping with a big star. So, maybe it was more about me than about us."

"And it's different with Asia? She's a lovely girl."

"Yeah, but I can't tell you why. I'm just so drawn to her. I can't explain it."

Mom pats my hand and opens her mouth to offer what I'm sure will be motherly wisdom, but the back door bursts open, and my eight-year-old niece, Janie, charges into the kitchen.

"Grandma, we're here."

"I can see that," Mom says.

"We brought an apple pie, a pumpkin pie, and a pecan pie." She wrinkles her nose. "And Mama cooked some collards. Yuck."

"What? Everybody likes collards," Mom says.

Janie frowns, then looks at me. "Even Aunt Davis?"

I make an extreme-yuck face until Mom turns to confront me. "Sure. I like collards."

"You've got pinkeye." Janie calls out to my brother and sister-in-law, who are coming through the back door, hands full of pies and a Crock-Pot. "Mom, Aunt Davis has pinkeye."

"I do not."

"Do so. That's exactly how my eye looked when I had it, and I couldn't play with any other kids until it got better."

"Do not." I can't believe I'm arguing with an eight-year-old. "I was chopping onions and got some juice in my eyes."

Janie is clearly unconvinced. "It's very contagious. Maybe you should go to your room and let Grandma bring you a plate."

I'm being bullied by a kid, so I'm relieved when Al and Asia return, each carrying a covered dish. "Asia, tell Janie I don't have pinkeye."

Janie eyes Asia with clear suspicion. "Who are you?"

"Janie!" my sister-in-law says. "Don't be rude."

Asia is unfazed. "I'm Davis's friend, and the person who washed the onion oil off her face and out of her eyes." She mirrors Janie's pose, hands on hips and leaning forward. "Who are you?"

Janie's eyebrows shoot skyward. "I'm her favorite niece."

"You're my only niece," I say. "Asia's directing the Christmas show. She even wrote the script."

"Really?" Janie's expression instantly changes from skeptical to awestruck. She's been hoping for a kid role she could audition for at the community theater. "Are there any child characters in your play?"

"Only a baby, and we're using a doll, not a real baby," Asia says.

"What about your next show?" Janie asks.

I share a look with Asia. We've avoided conversations about the future—mine and hers, and whether the Christmas Community Theater even has one. "Right now, we're just concentrating on the one that opens Saturday," I say.

Mom intuitively interrupts Janie's interrogation. "Janie,

how about setting the table. Your mom can get the plates and silverware for you."

I give Mom a grateful look and mouth "thank you." She replies with a quick, small smile. My brother, Bryan, and Al double-team carving the turkey and a small ham, while my sister-in-law is finding serving spoons and bowls for all the side dishes. We have so much food, there's barely room on the table for our plates.

Mom, never forgetting a lonely soul, had asked Ray, the widower who was cast as the rabbi in Asia's play, to join us, but he's spending Thanksgiving with his niece's family.

"I ran into Cora Lowenstein yesterday at the market," Mom says. "She said Joel is arriving here today, and he plans to stay for two weeks before he takes her back to New York with him for Hanukkah."

"Did you ask her about coming to the show?"

"I asked her to go with Al and me, and bring Joel along."

"What'd she say?" Asia's nearly crawling onto the kitchen island to get closer to hear Mom's answer.

"She's excited at the idea and said she'd do her best to get him to join us."

"When?" I'm nearly as excited as Asia.

"One day next week," Mom says, smiling.

❖

"This is our son. We don't have to give in to either of our parents," Trey, playing Michael, says.

"We should...should—" Sonya, playing Rebecca, stutters to a stop. "Shit. What's my line?"

The play opens in two days, and Sonya still hasn't learned the script. "But they are our parents—" I prompt her from my seat on the front row.

"But they are our parents, and they raised us okay," Sonya recites. "Maybe we should consider their traditions."

"Stop, stop, stop," Asia yells from her position a few seats down from me. We're sitting so that we view the stage from different angles to double-check the blocking of the stage action.

I shake my head. Sonya's delivery lacks emotion and enthusiasm. Even Trey looks frustrated at her performance.

Asia leverages herself onto the stage and walks over to Sonya. Her voice is low and scary calm. "We have only one more rehearsal before opening night. Where is your mind? Because it's not on this stage. Your delivery, when you remember your lines, is flat. Do I need to swap you with your understudy?"

Sonya sighs. "No." She rubs her forehead. "Sorry. I've had a crushing headache all day."

I'm not buying her story, and neither is Asia, judging from her body language. This is the first time Sonya's mentioned not feeling well and had actually been laughing and talking with several of the other cast members earlier.

"Let's just get through the rest of it, and then you can go home and nurse your headache." Asia hops off the stage and gives me a long look before we settle back into our seats.

❖

Asia is silent as I drive her home from the theater. Rehearsal did not go well. Sonya was distracted, which put everybody else's timing off. Dress rehearsal is tomorrow, their last chance to get it right before opening night.

Asia's head is down as I follow her up the outdoor staircase to her apartment, and she keeps staring at her feet when she turns to me after unlocking her door.

"I can't do this, Davis," she says.

"Sonya will be back on her game tomorrow, and you'll have a killer dress rehearsal." She seems uncharacteristically defeated, and I'm determined to do something, say something that will restore her confidence. I reach to lift her chin, but she looks sad when she finally meets my gaze, her eyes dull.

"I have to stop whatever's happening between us," she says. "I have to put my entire focus on the show. My career, my future, depends on it."

I'm flabbergasted. Totally didn't see this coming. "No. No. We're together on this. I care about the show, too. Let me help."

"Davis, honey." She pauses when she chokes on the endearment, the very word I grab onto as hope. "My every thought needs to be about the show, and you're a distraction. Besides, we both know this isn't going anywhere. My career is here on the East Coast, and yours will ultimately take you back to the West Coast, either for television or film jobs."

This can't be happening. I make a move to kiss away her doubts, but she stops me with a hand on my chest.

"Don't. This is hard enough, and I've made up my mind." She turns away, goes into her apartment, and closes the door behind her.

I stand frozen on the landing for several minutes. Should I pound on the door and demand she listen to reason? I raise my fist to do that, then stop. Asia has never responded well to pressure. I'll wait. The show will open successfully, and she'll relax. Then I'll reignite the fire between us, because chemistry does exist. Hot, explosive chemistry.

Still, her prediction nags at me. Are we destined to part at some point anyway because of our careers? My chest hurts at the thought of her leaving Christmas and the possibility of never seeing her again.

❖

The box office is open all today to sell tickets to tomorrow's opening. We have two shows—a matinee and an evening performance. Mom has sent me to buy four tickets for the evening performance Thursday, trusting that Cora will convince Joel to accompany her. There's no line, and the teen inside the glass booth looks bored.

"How are sales?" I ask after giving her my order.

"You're only about the tenth person to come in. Most are buying their tickets online," she says. "We're a long way from a sellout, but we've sold about half the seats."

History has taught us that shoppers hit the big-box stores on Black Friday, then come to Christmas for their specialty shopping over the weekend. That's why we decided Saturday was the best day to open the show. As people tire and decide a couple of hours in the theater would be a good break from shopping, they usually impulse-buy a number of tickets.

I pay for Mom's tickets, then purchase an opening-night one for myself before walking over to the auditorium door and finding it locked.

"It's locked because they're rehearsing," the teen says from the ticket booth. "They don't want anybody coming in to watch."

"I'm not anybody. I'm the acting coach." I try another door, but it's shut up tight too.

The girl shrugs. "They're all locked. You can bang on the door. I don't have a key. Or maybe you can text somebody to let you in."

I had wanted to sneak in and watch without Asia knowing I was there, so I shake my head. "They probably don't need me today anyway." Maybe I'll go to the coffee shop to drown my depression with an apple-caramel spice as I reminisce about the first time I saw Asia there.

CHAPTER FIFTEEN

I'm surprised to see Sonya in the coffee shop, sitting at a table with a guy sporting an unkept Jesus look. I put in my order, then walk to her table uninvited.

"Aren't you supposed to be at dress rehearsal?"

"I texted Asia that I quit."

I'm incredulous. "You texted her? You quit the day before the show opens?"

Sonya gives me a dismissive shrug. "She has an understudy for my part."

I take two mental deep breaths. "Why'd you do it?"

She indicates the man sitting across from her. "Roman has a part for me in a Broadway production he's casting." This entitled college student actually thinks she's going from college straight to a Broadway role. Sure, she has talent, but so do a lot of others who put in the work before getting their break.

Roman stands and holds out his hand. "You're Davis Hart."

My mom didn't raise me to be impolite, so I shake his hand. "Yes. Last time I looked in the mirror."

His smile is barely visible behind his untrimmed beard. "Man, I loved *Judge and Jury*, but I stopped watching when they killed off your character. You were the hottest actor on that show."

"Thank you." I offer a smile for his compliment. "What show are you casting for?"

"Well, it's not Broadway." He shifts his gaze between me and Sonya several times. "More like off-Broadway."

I pick up on the "like" right away. Off-Broadway, my ass. But Sonya doesn't seem to hear his hedging and probably won't listen if I expose him. So, I decide to try a different tactic.

"You have a starring role here," I tell Sonya. "Asia and the rest of the cast are depending on you to show up and do your very best. The success of this show might decide if the community theater ever opens another show in the future. And the entire town is depending on that theater to draw tourists into their shops, restaurants, and hotels."

"I have to think about my career." Sonya crosses her arms over her chest, obviously defiant. "I told Asia to find somebody who didn't care if they have a future in theater."

She's starting to piss me off. "You realize if you quit the show here, you'll fail the semester and won't graduate."

"I don't care."

"And you'll have to pay back the grant money you've been getting since you accepted the part."

Her eyes widen slightly, but she recovers quickly. "My daddy will pay it back. It wasn't that much."

I decide to embellish a bit. "Come to think of it, didn't you and Trey sign contracts to receive those stipends from the grant? I hope Daddy has deep pockets. You could be sued for breach of contract. Asia could claim pain and suffering caused by you pulling out the day before opening night, and the grant people could sue for damage to the show. Hell, the town might even be able to make a case for damages. Then, there are legal expenses and legal fees on top of that if you lose those lawsuits."

I see a flash of fear cross her features, but then she juts out her chin and narrows her eyes. "You're trying to scare me. Nobody's going to sue. He'll pay back the grant money, and that will take care of it."

"Take it from somebody who knows. Once word gets around that you had a starring role and ditched a show the day before it opens, you're toast in the business. One screwup and casting directors will pass right over you for someone who's proved they'll work hard and fulfill their contract like a professional. That goes double for unknown actors like you. I hate to see you blow your career before it ever starts."

Her brows draw together, eyes narrow, and her mouth flattens into a thin line while she listens. Then she literally growls out her words through her teeth. "Nobody is going to care about a little show in a community theater in a town that thinks it's Christmas year-round." She gathers her coat and purse, then heads for the door. "Come on, Roman. Let's get the rest of my things from my apartment and get the hell out of this town."

He rises more slowly, glancing at her, then me.

I shook my head. "Like off-Broadway?"

He shrugs. "Off-off-Broadway, but it is in the West Village. My friend has written a good script, and we've thrown our money together to sublet a stage from an improv company that's going on the road."

"She's sleeping with you, isn't she, to get the part?"

He scoffs. "More like I'm sleeping with her because she's dipping into her trust to help fund our show."

I wave him off. "Good luck with that. She does have acting talent, but you can't trust her. I'd get the money from her before you commit to spend it." I leave him, his mouth agape, to think over that possibility.

❖

I retrieve my caramel-apple spice that's been sitting on the counter during our conversation, but my favorite barista grabs it.

"That's probably not still warm. Want me to heat it for you?"

"Sure. Thanks." My usual small table in the corner is open, so I take my drink there and settle in to contemplate whether I should consider doing what Roman has planned—put on my own show to break back into the ranks of employed actors. But, like Roman, I will need money to back my own show. And I'm already short on cash.

The guy I sublet to in LA is almost two months behind on the rent, so I'm paying the landlord out of my pocket to keep my apartment. I also have to pay my Jeep lease, storage rent, and credit cards every month. So I've pretty much spent the advance money from the commercials I shot. Kylie had negotiated residuals if one shows on YouTube, but the insurance company hasn't released either commercial yet.

I've considered selling my jet ski, motorcycle, and other toys I have stored in Los Angles, but I'm too chicken to break the silence between me and Kylie, the only friend who would liquidate my stuff and go shake down my delinquent renter.

I'm not only getting desperate for a paying job, but I'm also growing restless.

When I lived in Los Angeles, I went to parties or hideaway, sex-filled weekends with Lisa. During breaks in shooting the series, I lunched with Kylie or others in the biz, surfed, snow-skied, and took part in a handful of other sports.

Now that Asia has cut me loose, it looks like I'm back to having dinner and watching television with Mom every night, and Al, too, most nights. It's only been a day, but I already miss picking up lunch to share with Asia while we go over stage blocking, lighting, and other stuff each day before rehearsal.

"Davis Hart, you old dog. I figured some jealous lover would have shot you dead by now."

I look up to see Butch Sanderson, former high school quarterback, staring down at me. He's filled out a bit, like most men when they hit their twenties, but not in a bad way yet. "Hey, Butch. Didn't recognize you in that suit and tie."

He shrugs and sits down without an invitation. "Football wasn't in the cards for me. Career-ending knee injury my freshman year in college."

"That sucks, man." I go along with his ridiculous implication that he could have had a career playing football. The only offers he got out of high school were from Division II colleges. "I'm sorry to hear that."

"I've managed to land on my feet, working at my dad's car dealership. Apparently, I have a talent for selling cars and managing the business." He gives me a pointed look. "I married Marley. We have a two-year-old boy, with a little girl on the way."

I sit back in my chair and smile, picking my words carefully. Butch and I had been rivals for Marley's affection back at Christmas High School. She hung on his arm at school but didn't care who knew she would slip off to get naked with me at every chance. Marley was only a bit of fun for me and is ancient history in my date book, so I'm happy to let him mark his territory now. "That's great. Tell Marley I said congratulations. I'm happy for you guys."

He grins. "I read your career isn't going all that well." He leans over the table toward me. "Still haven't learned to keep it in your pants, I guess."

I give him a nonchalant shrug, but inside I'm punching him in the mouth. "As always, there's another side to the story." I want to add that Marley wouldn't have jumped into bed with me the first time if he hadn't cheated on her with a cheerleader from our rival high school. But that's kid stuff now, so I let it go.

He sits back when he doesn't get a rise out of me. "So, what are you doing now?"

"This and that. Quick stuff because I came back East to help my mom recover from back surgery."

"Oh." He seems a little disappointed at this tame explanation, but then his smile widens again. "Wait…the cooking show." He slaps his knee. "That was hilarious. Marley and I watched that episode a million times. I mean, we know it had to be planned in a script or something, because all that stuff could never happen to one person in real life. That patch over your eye and those octopus legs hanging out of your mouth—" He's laughing so hard his face is pink and people at other tables are glancing our way.

"I know, right? They planned it, except the octopus legs hanging out of my mouth was my idea." It's just a little lie to preserve my dignity.

He dials down his laughter and wipes his eyes before looking at me again. "I'm not surprised. You always were a party animal." He pauses, as if an idea has just struck him. "Hey. We're having a get-together Sunday for Marley's birthday. Why don't you come? It'll mostly be people you know from high school." He points at me. "Your buddy, Tommy, and his husband, Bruce, will be there."

This surprises me. "I didn't know you and Tommy were friends. You weren't in high school."

"Yeah. I was an ass sometimes back then, wasn't I?" He waves dismissively. "We've all grown up. Bruce was my roommate at college, and we played on the football team together. He's a great guy."

I doubt Tommy and Bruce will attend, unless they come after Tommy is done at the evening show. A party does sound better than another exciting night of dinner on a TV tray while watching *Jeopardy* with Mom. "Maybe I will make it." I stand and point to the door. "Gotta run."

"We're going to throw burgers on the grill around seven, but people will start showing up as early as five." He quickly scribbles his address on a napkin, then hands it to me. "It'll be a great surprise for Marley if you can be there. Some of her new friends don't believe she knows you."

I hold up the napkin as confirmation that I have all the information needed to attend. "I'll try my best."

CHAPTER SIXTEEN

Opening night is terrible. Trey deserves a Tony Award for pretty much keeping pace with the understudy's ad-libbing when she couldn't remember her lines and changing his movements across the stage when she got hers wrong.

I wait two hours outside the theater for Asia, parked so I can see both the front of the theater and the backstage door. I'm determined to be her shoulder to cry on but fall asleep in my Jeep during the long wait. I'm jolted awake by loud tapping on the window next to my head. Asia, her bicycle at her side, is staring at me. No. She's frowning at me. I lower my window.

"Hey. How about a ride home? I can throw your bike in the back."

"Why are you here, Davis?"

"I saw the show tonight. I thought you might want to talk about it."

She snorts. "I don't need to talk about it. I need a lead actor who can remember her lines."

"She'll get better. It was just first-night jitters. I've been through those lines with her a million times. She knows the part."

"Maybe so, but at this point, I'm ready to dress Tommy in drag and let him play the role of Rebecca."

I open my door and start to get out. "Come on. It's cold. Let me drive you and your bike home."

She stiffens and backs up a few steps. "No, Davis. I meant

what I said. We have no future together, and I don't have time for anything that's just for fun."

"Asia—"

"Good night. Please don't follow me." She climbs onto her bicycle and heads off toward her apartment.

I get back into my Jeep and slam my fists on the steering wheel. "Damned hardheaded woman."

Her apartment is only about ten blocks away, but I follow anyway to make sure she arrives safely. I keep my distance, but the streets are nearly empty, so it's impossible to hide that I'm trailing her. I even park at the end of her driveway to watch until she's safely in her apartment. When she unlocks her door and walks inside without a glance my way, I realize I've been hoping for a little wave or a small smile. Hell. I'd have settled for a scowl to at least acknowledge my chivalry.

❖

"I thought you'd be hanging out at the theater every day," Mom says.

"I've seen that play so many times, I could play every part myself. I'm sick of it. At least in television, you're rehearsing and filming a different script every week." I shift my position on the sofa for the hundredth time. We've graduated from watching television in her bedroom to looking at it in the living room.

Mom eyes me. "Well, it doesn't appear I'm any more entertaining than Asia's show."

The mere mention of her name makes me want to growl. It also makes me want to cry. Instead, I stare at Mom belligerently.

"Go," she says. "Get some fresh air. Take a walk downtown. Do some window-shopping. I can't concentrate on this movie with you wallowing around on the sofa the entire time."

So she's kicking me out, too. "I'm fine."

"Were you this easily bored when you lived in LA?"

"No. I had lots of friends and parties to go to." Parties. Something nags at the back of my brain. Marley's birthday party! I sit up. "On second thought, I just remembered something I was invited to." I hope it's still going on. Butch said people would start arriving at five, and it's already eight thirty. Can't hurt to drive by and see, right?

❖

Cars and trucks line the street and fill the yard of the address Butch gave me. Good. The party isn't over. I don't bother to knock because the music's so loud, I can hear it from the street.

The house is larger than I'd expect a twenty-something to afford, but then, as his father's anointed successor, Butch likely has his career path paved for him after showing even the smallest talent for sales.

I weave my way through the crowd in the sunken living room to reach the patio, where I see Butch filling plastic cups from a beer keg, and Marley holding court with a group of women. She spots me first.

"As I live and breathe. Davis Hart."

I open my arms in a "here in the flesh" gesture and smile when everyone within hearing distance turns to stare. "The one and only," I say.

She rushes over to hug me. Except for her pregnant belly, she doesn't look much different, but I'm very aware that I do. I've let my hair grow out from the short style I wore in high school and college, and muscles have changed my body from painfully thin to athletically lean. She releases me from the prolonged hug, then holds me at arm's length.

"Wow. You look better than ever."

"Thanks. You haven't aged a bit. Still the beauty queen."

She pulls a face. "I feel like a cow."

"When are you due?"

"Two more months." She hooks her arm in mine and leads me to a couple of chairs a few feet away from the patio crowd. The women she was talking with are glancing our way and whispering among themselves. I recognize a couple of them from high school, so I give them a little wave to let them know I see them looking.

"So, what are you doing now that you're out of college?"

She does a this-and-that gesture with her head, then glances over at Butch. "We married pretty much as soon as we graduated, and then I started a little business selling some purses I made on Etsy. It let me work at home and set my own schedule while Butch was trying to establish himself in the car business."

"You always were artistic and had a flair for fashion. You don't still do that?"

"No. I immediately got pregnant, and once the baby was born, he took up all my time."

I scan the yard. "Is he around? He must be nearly five now."

"He's four, almost five. Mama took him home with her for the night once the liquor started flowing and the music got loud."

"So, you're a stay-at-home mom now?"

"Yep. It's a full-time job, even with the maid who comes in twice a week to help with the housework. And I fill in for Butch's dealership receptionist when she's off or out sick."

Butch walks up. "Don't worry. She kept the financial records of the Etsy business she gave up, and she tracks the unpaid hours she puts in at the dealership. She would pretty much have me by the balls if I ever thought about divorcing her or cheating." He hands me a cup of beer and pulls another chair over to join us. "As if I'd want to. She's the light of my life and my support system. I'd be lost without her." He reaches for Marley's hand, which I read as a gesture of possession until I see Marley's affection for him in her eyes.

"He's a good husband," she says.

I'm strangely warmed. "That's really great, you guys. Looks like we've all come a long way since high school."

Marley tilts her head. "Really? The Hollywood gossip rags say you're still cattin' around just like you did back then."

I guess Marley's over her infatuation with me, but not the fact that I wasn't exclusive while we were sleeping together.

I nod, wanting to be truthful. "I learned a hard lesson. I'm looking to do some theater."

Finally, some others I'd known in high school drift over to say hello. Most seem awestruck. Others apparently aren't.

"So, did you come back here because you've already slept with all the women on the West Coast?" A man I don't recognize is apparently the spokesman for a group of three, all dressed in khaki shorts and deck shoes, even though Butch's outdoor propane heaters aren't doing much to ward off the night's increasing chill. "Just kidding," he says. In contrast to the challenge of his greeting, he holds out a fresh cup of beer to replace my now-empty one.

Wordlessly, I accept the beer, still deciding how to respond when he turns to Butch to discuss news of a golf-course upgrade for the next ten minutes, as if he hadn't said anything even vaguely offensive to me. I opt to ignore his earlier rude remark, until his chat about golf ends and he turns to me again.

"Did you really eat out Lisa Langston? Damn, she's hot. I wouldn't mind her dancing on my pole." He laughs and elbows his buddies, who laugh with him. His sidekicks are obviously drunk.

I stand, because I'm just shy of six feet tall and have at least an inch on the tallest of the trio. "First of all, that's none of your business. Secondly, I take offense at your crass, juvenile choice of words, but I'm going to excuse your poor manners because you can't be held responsible for your family's obvious inbreeding."

He moves within a step of me, pushing his face up close to mine. "At least we don't have any queers in our family." He steps back when I take a half step to nearly close the space between us.

Marley stands, and the threatening threesome all take another step backward. It's interesting that they appear afraid of her. "Butch, it's time for those three to go home." Her words drip ice, and Butch jumps up.

"Come on now, Josh. Y'all don't have to go home, but you can't stay out here and ruin Marley's birthday." Butch ushers his friends into the house.

Before they go inside, Josh wrestles free of Butch's loose grip and turns back to us. "Lezzie bitch thinks she's better than the rest of us because she was on TV." Butch grabs him again to drag him toward the house, but Josh shakes him off. "I don't know why I have to leave. She's the one showing up here to sniff around your wife. After all, she ain't had a taste of that pussy since high school. Or did Marley keep handing it out while you were in—"

Butch's fist cuts Josh's rant short. He stares down at Josh, now laid out on the grass, and flexes his hand. "Damn, his jaw is hard." He looks to the other two men, who appear stunned. "Take him home to sleep it off. All of you sober up. I'll deal with you at work tomorrow." He waves them toward the door. "I said get out." He follows them into the house, probably to make sure they leave.

I sit down again and rub my face, because I'm feeling strangely woozy. "Sorry. Maybe I shouldn't have come."

Marley's hand is on my arm, and it anchors my swimming head for a moment. "No. I'm glad you did. I'm sorry Butch's stupid friends ruined our visit. They all work at the dealership."

"Don't worry about it. I've weathered a lot worse from social-media trolls." I stand and sway a bit. "But, you know, I think I'm going to leave now."

"Oh, no. You just got here." Marley grabs my arm to steady me. "Are you sure you're okay to drive home?"

"I haven't even had two beers, but I don't feel so great. Maybe I'm coming down with something."

Marley holds me up as I weave toward the door. "I don't

know, Davis. Let me call you an Uber. Maybe you have a case of vertigo."

A guy I don't recognize opens the door as we start to enter the house. "Hey, if you need a ride, I was about to leave. I'd be happy to drop you off wherever." He holds his hand out. "Hi. I'm Doug. You don't know me, but I'm the new salesman at Butch's dealership and a big fan of yours."

"Doug, that would be awesome," Marley says. "Butch can have her Jeep delivered to Mrs. Hart's house tomorrow."

My head is seriously swimming, so I have no choice but to accept. "Okay." I recite the address as Marley helps me into Doug's truck.

Doug starts it and puts it into gear. "You know, I do a little acting myself."

I prop against the door, resting my head against the cool window. "Really?" I close my eyes as the landscape whips and swirls past.

"Yeah. I'm the wiener mascot for Pop's Big Dog."

Pop's is a regional fast-food restaurant known for its menu of gourmet hot dogs. There's even talk of it going national. "You dress up like a big hot dog?" I can't believe this guy is equating his role as a giant hot dog with my professional acting.

"Yep. I'm not saying it's acting like you do, but it's tougher than you'd think."

"I'm sure." My eyes are very heavy, and my last thought is that I really want to sleep.

"I've just got one quick stop to make. Then I'll take you home."

❖

"Davis. Davis. Wake up." I don't want to wake up, but someone is shaking my shoulders. "What the hell are you wearing?" Everything's fuzzy, but Asia's voice filters through my fog. "We need to get you out of here."

"Where am I?"

"You're in the drunk tank at the county jail. Tommy's seeing what we have to do to get you released." Asia's tone is stern.

"Wh-what? How did I get here?" I try to sit up, but something bulky is between my legs, like a third leg or a huge dick.

"That's the million-dollar question." Asia sounds annoyed. "I take that back. The million-dollar question is where you found this hot-dog costume you're wearing."

"Wha-what?" I keep trying to get up, but I only manage to roll off the narrow cot that's attached to the wall and hit the floor with a soft thump. Lots of padding in this thing.

She grabs my arms and jerks me up. "Let's get it off and hope you have clothes under it." She seems impatient as she searches the costume, finally finding a hidden zipper in the front. We struggle to get me out of it. "Stop, stop, stop," she says. "Put your head as far as it can go in the top, then step out of the leg holes at the bottom." She jerks the costume down so my head's above the face hole, then places my hand on her shoulder for balance.

I panic when my head is suddenly encased in thick padding and total darkness. "Mmmp. Can't breathe, can't breathe." My breath is coming in quick, short pants. I'm hyperventilating. *Deep breaths. Deep breaths.* But I can't breathe well because my heart is racing.

"Hold your breath and lift your right foot." She guides it free. "Now the left. The quicker you do this, the sooner we can get your head out."

The last of her words fades into silence and blackness.

"What'd you do to her? She was fine when I checked on her just a few minutes before you guys got here."

I blink at the source of the deep voice. Bruce? The big, but nice, lump of muscle that was the football center for our high school, and is now Tommy's husband, is dressed in a deputy's uniform.

"Asia said she was helping her get out of that hot-dog

costume, and she started to hyperventilate when her head got stuck in the top of it."

"Tommy?" I can only manage a hoarse whisper. I close my eyes and try to swallow to lubricate my throat before I try to speak again. I should have opened my mouth, and then maybe some of the cup of cold water thrown at my face would have gone inside.

"That should sober her up some," Asia says.

Sputtering, I sit up. I'm still dizzy and lean against the bars of my temporary quarters as Tommy helps me stand.

"She's not drunk," Bruce says. "They took her by the hospital to have her checked out, and they drew blood to see what was in her system in case they had to administer any life-saving drugs. They found only a trace of alcohol, but she tested positive for Rohypnol."

"What's that?" Tommy asks.

My head's starting to clear a little. "I was roofied?"

"It's a date-rape drug," Asia says, the bitterness in her voice no longer directed at me. "Did they—"

Bruce shakes his head. "The doc said she hasn't been sexually assaulted."

"So, that's why I didn't have to pay bail to get her out?" Tommy asks.

"Oh, she's not under arrest," Bruce says. "I thought she might want to sleep some of it off while I figured out who to call to take her home."

"Who did this to her?" Asia looks ready to kill, and Bruce takes a step back. I'm thinking I might want to do the same.

"It was pretty easy to track down the culprits since only one guy in town has that costume and the keys to the Pop's Big-Dog-mobile. He implicated three other guys, and they all said it was just a prank, that they didn't mean for her to end up in a wreck."

"I was in a wreck?" Damn, my head hurts.

"Yeah, but the doc said that other than a few bruises, you weren't injured. He said you might be a little sore for a few days, but that suit has a lot of padding." Bruce frowns. "I can arrest them, but it would require paperwork the media might pick up. I didn't know if you'd want the publicity."

Asia answers for me. "No. She doesn't."

I finally find my tongue. "Thanks, Bruce."

"Thanks, baby. We'll take her home, and I'll see you later." Tommy gives his husband a quick kiss, then tries to steady me as we head down the hallway to the exit, but his slight build isn't enough to support my weight.

"Let me help." Bruce slips my arm over his broad shoulders and easily bears my weight. "Can't have you fall on our steps and bust something. The sheriff's department doesn't like publicity either."

❖

I close my eyes against the blur of the passing landscape and find the motion of my Jeep strangely comforting. Asia is driving, while Tommy follows in his car. "How did you know to come for me?"

"Bruce called your mother, and she phoned me. Tommy and I were still at the theater, so he offered to pick you up. I came along so we could retrieve your Jeep from the party, too."

I rub my forehead with the heel of my hand. "The last thing I can remember is Marley offering to call an Uber for me. I only drank two beers, and I didn't even finish the second one." I open my eyes and squint at her briefly before the motion outside her window makes me dizzy and I close my eyes again. "Do you know what happened?"

"Apparently, a group of guys at the party thought it'd be funny to drug you, dress you in that hot-dog costume, and shoot videos of you standing next to that vehicle that looks like a big hot dog. It was parked in front of a restaurant that had a fifteen-foot plastic chicken out front."

"Oh, no. The Red Rooster, Pop's biggest competition."

"Bruce said they'd quit serving inside, so most of the customers were already gone, and I doubt anyone who was there recognized you in that ridiculous wiener getup."

"How did I get in a wreck?" I'm trying to piece this weird situation together since my mind's still blank.

"The guys didn't realize the keys were in the vehicle, or anticipate that you'd suddenly decide you needed to go home and try to drive the hot dog out of the parking lot."

I hold my head in both hands. "How far did I go? I didn't hurt anybody, did I?"

"You're lucky you weren't charged with chicken-cide." We pull to a stop in Mom's driveway. I'm leaning against the door, so Tommy catches me when he opens it and I fall out.

"What is chicken-cide?"

"You murdered The Red Rooster's fifteen-foot chicken that stands out front. Flattened it with your hot-dog-mobile. The chicken is just splinters of plastic now," Tommy says.

Mom is already opening the door and hobbling out onto the porch. "Is she okay?"

"Don't come down the steps, Ida. You might fall," Asia says. "She's fine. Just needs to sleep it off."

She and Tommy each take one of my arms over their shoulders because my legs are very weak and wobbly. They guide me inside, while Mom opens doors and points the way to my bedroom.

"I was so worried," Mom says. "Thank you both for bringing her home. I'm not cleared to drive yet, and Al doesn't see well at night."

I sink onto the soft oblivion of my bed, and then a sudden, catastrophic thought hits me. *If they post this online, what's left of my career is ashes.* I struggle to get up, fighting against the blanket Asia is trying to drape over me. I can't stop the tears streaming down my face. "I'll be a laughingstock. I'll never act again."

Tommy, his hands on my shoulders, holds me down until I

quit thrashing and sob. "I'm going to call Kylie," Tommy says. "She'll know what to do."

"Kylie hates me. She won't help. She's not my agent anymore." I'm wailing now.

"I'll talk to her, honey." Mom strokes my hair to console me.

Asia shoos them out of the room. "You guys go make the call, and I'll get her undressed and under the covers."

"You hate me, too." I'm still wailing.

"You're an idiot, but I don't hate you." She pulls me into a sitting position and tugs my shirt over my head like she's undressing a baby. I'm hot and clammy with sweat—a side effect of the roofie—so I pull off my sports bra, too.

"Can you stand up to get your pants off, or do you need to lie down?"

I flop back onto the bed. "I'm sorry. I don't think I'm up for sex right now." This is a drugged admission, not a tease.

She snorts as she removes my shoes and shorts, leaving my underwear. "I'm trying to get you undressed and under the covers so you can sleep this off. Do you have pajamas, or do you sleep in a T-shirt?"

"Too hot. Sweating." My voice sounds far away as my eyelids grow very heavy.

"I'll turn on the ceiling fan," she says.

"Okay." I close my eyes and feel the sheet, cool against my skin, as she covers me. "Asia?"

"I'm still here." Her fingers brush against my cheek.

"I screwed up."

Her fingers touch my lips to still them. "This fiasco tonight isn't your fault."

"No. Not that. I screwed up and fell in love with you."

"Oh, Davis."

My confession made, I sink into a deep, drug-induced sleep.

CHAPTER SEVENTEEN

"You need to eat something more than toast." Mom places a glass of orange juice next to the toast she's buttered for me. "Let me make you some eggs."

"Ugh. The thought of eggs makes me want to hurl."

"How about some cheese grits? You love cheese grits." Mom's cell phone rings, and she walks to the other end of the kitchen island to retrieve it. "Hello? Hey, sweetie. She's right here. Why don't you FaceTime her? She has her phone next to her. I'm making her something to eat, and my phone is telling me that Al is trying to call."

I'm waving my hands to tell Mom I don't want to talk to anybody, but she switches calls, and my phone beeps to indicate I have a Facetime call from Kylie waiting.

"Mom!"

She waves off my protest and walks into her bedroom to talk to Al in private.

I stare at my phone, then finally swipe to answer. "Kylie? Are you okay?" She's looking a little haggard.

"Before you say anything, Ida called and told me about some guys drugging you and setting you up as a prank."

"Oh, God." I put my hands over my face. "I'm sorry."

There's a long pause before she speaks, sounding sad. "Sorry for what, Davis?"

I drop my hands. "I'm sorry for everything—for doubting you, for yelling at you, for firing you. I'm sorry I treated you like an employee instead of a friend. And I'm sorry Mom called you after I treated you so badly."

"Thank you. As much as I've missed you, I needed to hear that apology."

"I miss you so much. You've been my best friend for so many years. I have no idea how you've put up with me and my stupid ego."

She chuckles softly and shakes her head. "I don't know either." She pauses again. "But I do know that if what happened to you gets out, it will hurt your career, even though you're the victim. The online trolls will say that's what you get for being such a party animal, drinking and carousing so much."

"I don't care what they say about me. I'm worried they'll come to Christmas and snoop around to get more dirt on me. I've been seen all over town with Asia, and she doesn't deserve to get tangled up in my bad publicity."

There's a long silence as Kylie stares at me over our video connection. "Damn, Davis. Don't take this the wrong way, but you've never been concerned about collateral damage from your escapades before now. I'm afraid, Peter Pan, that she's your Wendy, and you're finally growing up."

"If I have to throw myself under the bus and go back to LA to take the paparazzi off her trail, I will. I don't want to go, but I don't know what else to do."

"No need to pack your bags. I've taken care of everything. A lawyer from the city will meet with the four men at the district attorney's office this afternoon. The hot-dog guy will sign a statement taking responsibility for damages to his employer's vehicle. The other three will sign statements admitting they conspired to drug your beer, then dressed you in that costume while you were incoherent and helped you into the vehicle where the keys were in the ignition. They'll also have to hand over their phones to have any videos or photos deleted, and to be checked to make sure nothing has been uploaded to a cloud somewhere without being deleted."

"Why would they agree to that?"

"Because drugging you is a criminal offense that could send them to prison for several years. That's a much bigger threat than a civil suit. The four of them probably don't have enough assets to pay for attorney fees, much less damages you'd suffer if any photo or video happens to appear on social media."

"If you have them confessing in front of the DA, she'll file charges for sure, and the media will be crawling all over any trial that would follow. I feel stupid enough without dragging the whole incident out before the public."

"The DA is a friend of mine and will keep their confessions in her home safe. She won't file charges unless someone leaks a photo or video to the public."

"What about the people who were in the restaurant?"

"They don't have any security cameras in the parking lot, and no other business is close enough to have caught anything on theirs. Plus, I seriously doubt anyone recognized you in that hot-dog costume. It was pretty dark where you were, and only your face was sticking out." She looks down, but I can see she's trying not to smile. "Only two people have a photo of you in that costume."

I groaned. "Who? I have to know."

She looks up again but doesn't hide her grin. "Me and Tommy. He got a quick shot of you in the jail cell."

I cover my face with my hands again. "I'm never going to live this down, am I?"

"Nope," she says, still smiling.

I rub my cheek. "Okay. Do I need to be at the meeting?"

"You don't have to go, but you can if you want to see those guys grovel. The attorney is a friend of Phil's and looks and talks like he works for the mafia."

"So does Phil."

She laughs that Kylie laugh I've missed so much. "Yeah, he

does. Oh, and Phil might call you later this week. He could have a lead on a job for you."

"I really like Phil, but I want you to be my agent, and I don't think I can afford both of you."

She shakes her head. "How stupid do you think I am?"

"You're not stupid. I've never said you were stupid."

"That's why I'm still, and have always been, your agent. You might have verbally fired me, but I have a contract with you that says you have to fire me in writing."

"I need to call Phil, then. But damn. What if he has a job for me?"

"Phil is my uncle, married to my mother's sister. He was a top agent with the agency I work under but retired five years ago. He's been working with you only as a favor to me. I've tried to pay him, of course, but he doesn't need the money and refuses to take it."

"You sent Phil to me?" I don't hide the tears streaming down my cheeks, and I choke out my next words. "I'm such a bad friend. I love you, ya know. Like the sister I've never had."

Her eyes also turn watery. "I know. I love you, too. Like a third sister, because I already have two."

We both wipe our faces and laugh. We've confessed these same endearments many times during our long friendship, but the sentiment never has seemed more real, more important than at this very moment.

❖

"You can sing and dance, can't you?" Phil's gruff question almost sounds like an accusation, but I don't take it personally. That's just Phil.

"Duh. I wouldn't be looking for a Broadway role if I couldn't."

"I know some people who have a script drawn from a lesbian comic strip. It's a book, actually, but started as a comic strip. They've got the backing to produce it off-Broadway. I heard they're putting a cast together, so I want to know if you're interested before I chase them down and see if I can get you an audition."

"That would be so great!" I hesitate. "But wouldn't that typecast me in lesbian roles—of which there aren't many—considering it's already well-publicized that I am gay? It might be better for my career to snag a role in something like *Chicago*, where the female cast members wear fishnet stockings and not much else."

"Sure, we can wait for something like that in one of the traveling troupes, but you might be broke and completely forgotten by the time it comes around. Besides, you don't have the body type they look for to cast those dancers." He coughs, sounding like he's going to hack up a lung. "Have you completely dismissed TV roles? They film a lot of shows on the East Coast now."

"I want to get back to theater."

"Okay, kid. I'll keep working my contacts. I'll call you in a couple days."

I end the conversation with Phil and open my laptop. I'm dying to see Asia's show again, hoping the Rebecca understudy is improving. I should stay away from her in case the hot-dog incident does go public, but I'm desperate to be near her, even if she doesn't know I'm there. Today's Monday, when most theaters are closed, so I buy a seat on the back row of Tuesday night's show. If I wear a ball cap and sneak in after it starts, nobody will know I'm there.

❖

I'm restless. I stayed home last night and watched television with Mom and Al after Kylie called to confirm that all four of my kidnappers had signed nondisclosure agreements and surrendered their phones for examination. What's more, three of the four worked for Butch, and he fired all of them. Butch apparently doesn't hold a grudge from high school, and I was glad to know Marley is happily married to a decent guy. Kylie assured me that only Butch and Marley knew I'd been drugged, and I didn't have any reason to worry about them talking because they were concerned their social standing would suffer if people knew it had happened at their party.

Still, I'm reluctant to leave the house, held prisoner by the fear that someone around town will see me and put me and the hot-dog incident together. So, I'm relieved when Tommy drops by for a visit.

He gives Mom a big hug. "Hi, Mrs. H. Are you feeling okay since your back surgery?"

Mom kisses him on the cheek. "I'm doing very well. I've been cleared to resume my water-aerobics class at the Y, and it's helping me loosen everything that got stiff while I was lying around all day."

"That's so good to hear." He hands over something wrapped in a red-checked cloth napkin. "Bruce got me a bread maker, so I've been baking up a storm. I brought you a loaf I made this morning. It's still warm."

Mom's eyes light up when he hands it over. "I love fresh bread. Davis, get some plates and the butter."

I hurry to grab some small plates, a couple of butter knives, and the butter dish. Tommy, having spent much of his childhood at my house, goes directly to the drawer where Mom keeps her bread knife. In less than a minute, we're all moaning our approval of Tommy's bread-making skills.

"You feeling better?" This question is for me, not Mom.

"Yeah. I still have a small headache, but it's almost gone." I stare down at my second slice of buttered bread. "It's really scary to realize how easy it is for someone to drug you." I look back up at Tommy. "I can't remember anything after that guy offered to give me a ride home. Absolutely nothing. It's all a blank until when you and Asia woke me up in that jail cell."

Mom rises from her seat and comes over to hug me. "I'm so glad nothing really bad happened to you." Her words are choked, and tears fill her eyes. A second knock at the door draws her attention. "That's Al. He's taking me to the Y for my water aerobics class." She kisses the top of my head. "See you later, kids."

"I know it's absolutely imperative to keep this quiet, but I wish I could tell everyone in town to watch out for these guys," Tommy says after Mom leaves. "Why did they have a roofie anyway, unless they intended to drug some unsuspecting girl and do who knows what to her?"

I'm ready for a change of subject. "So, I've got a ticket for tonight's show."

"Does Asia know?"

"No. I'm planning to sneak in after the play starts and sit on the back row. I'm still not sure someone might leak something about last night, and I don't want her to get tainted by my crap."

We're both quiet for a few minutes, pretending to be absorbed in eating our bread. Finally, I can't hold back my question.

"Have you talked to her today? Is she mad at me?"

Tommy chews a moment longer, and his answer is careful. "She's not angry, but she's cautious. Something from last night could pop up on social media days, or even a week from now, and go viral. The show isn't going all that well. The understudy playing Rebecca is okay, but her performance is entirely forgettable, and that critic is supposed to show up Thursday night. She's worried that if your incident becomes public, her association with you will completely overshadow what she's trying to do."

"So, I guess she's pretty stressed."

"She has no plan B if this show isn't successful enough to get her some career cred or at least draw adequate interest to secure funding for another show here after this one." Tommy left his seat to wrap his arms around me. "You can go to the show tonight, but I'm glad you aren't planning to try to talk to her."

My eyes begin to tear again, and I wonder briefly if the

rawness of my emotions is an after-effect of the roofie. "It's hard to stay away from her...especially now when she needs support, someone in her camp to cheer her on." I rub the very real ache in my chest. "It hurts to not be there for her."

"I know, honey." He hugs me even tighter. "I'll make sure she knows that, and I'll have her back for you."

"Thanks, man. You and Kylie are the best friends anyone can have."

He releases me and sits again, his eyes bright and his expression hopeful. "You talked to Kylie?"

"Yeah." I wipe my eyes and smile. "We made up. I mean, I apologized for firing her, and she informed me that she was never really fired. She was just giving me the silent treatment to let me feel what it would be like if she wasn't my agent. Turns out that Phil is her uncle and was covering for her." I could tell by his expression he already knows about Phil.

"That's so great. I'm glad you two made up."

I scoff. "Be real. You were on her side from the beginning."

"You were being an entitled brat." He buffs his fingernails against his shoulder in an arrogant gesture. "You're lucky I talked her out of tearing up her contract and persuaded her to wait for you to come around." He gives me a cocky look. "Did she make you grovel? I told her to do that before she admitted that you hadn't legally fired her."

"No." I swat at him. "Now who's being a brat?"

He grins. "But you still love me."

"Yes. I do." I laugh, cheered by my playful friend. "And, for the record, I groveled before she had a chance to make me."

"Even better." He squirms as if settling in his seat. "So, what did the lawyer say about how the meeting went with the district attorney? I want all the dirt."

CHAPTER EIGHTEEN

I sink into my seat and tug the bill of my ball cap lower. The theater is only about half full, and the understudy's performance was as flat as a Texas blacktop. Although the average theatergoer probably wouldn't pick up on it, I can clearly read frustration all over Trey's face as he tries to turn in a good performance next to her lackluster one. It was torture to watch, and I'm regretting my part in getting tickets for Joel Lowenstein and his mother for later this week. Hopefully, after he sees the play, he won't use the opportunity to explain why community theater shouldn't discourage people from spending money to see a professionally produced and acted show.

I stand and can't help but glance at the lighting booth behind the last seats when I take a second to stretch the kinks out of my too-long legs. I grow still when Asia and I look at each other, but then my chest cramps when she turns away as though I'm nobody.

After I slink out of the theater, I head straight for my Jeep and drive aimlessly because I don't want to go home and answer a barrage of questions from Mom about the show, then finally park on the north edge of downtown. I wind my way through the trees, remembering how warm Asia's hand felt in mine when we took this path together only weeks before. Then I settle onto the same bench where we had gazed at the sky, but tonight's cloud cover is blocking out the starry night we'd enjoyed together. Even more prophetic, a handwritten sign hangs over the utility box for the pond's Santa's sleigh feature—*Out of Order*.

I'm now in full gloom.

❖

It's very late or, rather, very early in the morning when I finally return home.

"Davis?" Mom, who sounds wide awake, calls out from the bedroom. "Is that you?"

"Yeah. Sorry. I was trying to be quiet so I wouldn't bother you."

"I was worried when you didn't come home after the play. Did you see Asia tonight?"

"Yeah…saw her, but I didn't talk to her." I toss my keys onto the kitchen island and open the refrigerator to stare inside. I'm not hungry, but I finally take out a carton of milk and pour myself a small glass.

Mom hobbles in from her bedroom. "Did she see you?"

"Yes. She saw me."

Mom gives an impatient huff. "Did you try to talk to her?"

"No. She was in the lighting booth, and it's soundproof."

Mom goes to the kitchen junk drawer and grumbles as she rummages through the assortment of items there. "I know there must be some pliers here somewhere."

I sigh and down the last of my milk. "Why in God's name do you need pliers at three in the morning?" I go over to help her look, but she turns to me.

"Because getting information out of you is like pulling teeth, and I'm going to pull a few more if you don't tell me everything."

I tamp down the urge to get a second glass and pour myself some brandy this time. "I snuck into the theater when they dimmed the lights for the first act, then waited until almost everyone was gone to leave so nobody would recognize me. When I stood up and glanced toward the lighting booth, Asia looked directly at me for a few seconds. Then she turned away like she didn't know me."

"Maybe she didn't really see you, but was just looking toward you."

"We stared at each other a few seconds before she turned her back to me."

"Oh, honey. You know why. You and Tommy talked about it earlier. How was the play?"

I hang my head. "The understudy sucks. Trey tries his best to make up for her flat performance, but he can only do so much. I'm sorry we arranged for Mrs. Lowenstein to take Joel to see it on Thursday."

Mom pats my arm, but yawns. "Sometimes when everything looks bleak, you figure out later that it was just the dark before the dawn. Go to bed. I won't be able to sleep if you're rummaging around the house."

We both know that isn't true—she can sleep through a booming thunderstorm—but it's the push I need toward the solitude of my childhood bedroom to sort through my feelings and my future.

❖

"We're done." Tommy comes through the back door without knocking. "The play is closing."

Mom and I look up from our lunch after sleeping right through the breakfast hours.

"What?" I'm sure I've heard wrong.

"We have tickets for tomorrow night," Mom says.

"Sonya's understudy wasn't the best, but now we don't even have her."

"She quit?" I'm incredulous. Is the generation behind me so self-involved they don't care how their lack of commitment affects others? "Death or prison are the only acceptable excuses."

Tommy sighs. "Her mother died."

"Oh, that poor girl," Mom says.

Tommy nods. "It's not a matter of just going to a funeral and taking some time off to grieve. She doesn't know when she'll be back. Her father has cancer, and her mother was his caregiver. He's stage four but could live two to three more months. He already has home hospice care and all his doctors established there, so coming here and disrupting all that in his final months isn't practical."

"Who else can play the part?" Mom asks.

"Nobody," Tommy says. "Even if we shut down for a few weeks and reopen closer to the holidays, that's not enough time to audition actors and get someone up to speed with the script and stage blocking."

"I can do it." I surprise myself by blurting out this fact without a single preceding thought.

They both stare at me like I've grown horns.

"What? I know all the lines, the blocking, everything." I'm warming to the idea as I try to convince them. "I coached Sonya and her understudy through the role. I could walk onstage and do it right now."

Tommy is shaking his head. "Have you forgotten they can't pay you? Not even scale."

"What's scale?" Mom looks confused. "She would do it free for Asia."

"Don't be a grinch, Tommy." I'd see the hand of God in this opportunity if I was religious. At the very least, I believe karma is giving me a chance to redeem my selfish life. "You know a lot of those big movie stars must donate their time and talent to some worthy causes. This is a worthy cause. We're trying to save Christmas—the town, not the holiday."

He's quiet for a few seconds as his expression changes from glum to very serious. "Asia is convinced that a professional association with you will hurt her career more than help. I doubt today's situation will change her perspective."

"Well, you won't know if Davis doesn't talk to her." Mom glares at Tommy. She obviously supports my idea.

"I'm planning to go do just that right now." I take the last bite of my sandwich and put my dishes in the dishwasher. "Is she at the theater this morning?"

"She was thirty minutes ago. I don't know if she's still there," Tommy says. "Want me to go with you?"

I take a few seconds to consider his offer. "No. I think I need to talk to her by myself." My phone chimes to indicate an incoming FaceTime request as I grab my jacket from its hook by the back door. I tap the screen to open the app. "Hey, Kylie. I don't have time to talk right now. Can I call you back in an hour or two?" I wave good-bye to Mom and Tommy as I head out to my Jeep.

"No. You're going to want to talk to me right now." Her grin is wide, so I'm pretty sure it's not bad news like maybe a video of me drugged up and wearing a hot-dog costume showed up online.

"What's up?" Her smile makes me smile back at her. Or maybe it's just that I'm so happy to be on my way to talk with Asia.

"You need to get in your Jeep now and drive to New York. I'll text you the address and the person to ask for."

"An audition?"

"They might ask you to read, but they already want you."

I stop in the driveway, next to the Jeep. "Broadway?" My heart is racing now.

Her smile dims a little, and she shrugs. "Not Broadway, but a better opportunity than off-Broadway."

"Come on. Spill. I really am in a hurry."

"A new television series." She tilts her head back and forth a few times in her "sort of" gesture. "It's a pilot for a series that's being produced by Sandra Rawls, so it's sure to be a hit. They expect this one to fill a slot behind one of her current hit shows and that there will be crossovers between them."

Wow. Sandra Rawls. She currently has no less than six hit shows pulling in top ratings. Everything she touches seems to turn to gold—at the bank and the award shows. I climb into my Jeep. "What's the role?"

"You'd play a young technology-savvy female detective partnered with a legendary, but old, male detective, who the department wants to discreetly push into retirement because he isn't receptive to new methods and things like sexual harassment and diversity training. The show is tentatively titled *District 12*. This role is meant for you."

She's right, but I still can't ignore the big issue. "Let me guess. They feel safe casting me because there's no chance I'll sleep with my costar." I place my phone in the holder so I can start my Jeep to back out of the driveway.

"Don't be bitter. Nobody has said that." Kylie shuffles some papers on her desk, then begins typing on her phone. "I'm texting you the address. They'd like to see you this morning if you can get there in the next ninety minutes."

"I have something I need to do right now, but I can leave for the city right after that."

"How long will it take?"

"I don't know. Maybe about thirty minutes."

"How far are you from the city?"

"A little over an hour."

"That would be cutting it close. They've got a plane to catch. I'll let them know you're on the way." She pauses, staring hard at me over our video connection. "Don't miss this meeting, Davis. The part is perfect for you. If you weren't already off *Judge and Jury*, I'd recommend you find a way out of that contract to take this new role."

"I hear you. I'll make the meeting." I end our call and careen around a corner in my rush to get to the theater.

❖

I bang on the backstage door until my hand hurts, then go around to the glassed entrance and bang on that door. Finally, a member of the janitorial company that cleans the theater daily comes to let me in. "Thanks, man. Is Asia here?"

"Miss Asia is in the sound booth." He uses his keys to relock the door after me. "Where have you been? She's been very sad since you quit coming to help."

"It's a long, complicated story, but she's the one who kicked me out. I'm hoping to talk her into letting me come back."

He nods. "That would be good. They're saying the show is in trouble."

"I'm hoping to fix that." Hurrying through the doors to the auditorium, I'm relieved to see she's still there. I fling open the door to the sound booth, but she doesn't look up at me.

"What are you doing here, Davis?" She pretends to be busy with the lighting controls, flipping a stage light on and off and adjusting the intensity of the spotlight.

"Tommy said you need an actor for the Rebecca role."

She looks up now, her gaze questioning. "You know someone?"

"Me."

She scoffs. "Be real."

"I am. I already know the part. I've coached two actors through it."

"Let's see, how many reasons are there that this is not a good idea?" She holds up her hand to tick each off one and looks up as if reading from writing on the ceiling. "I can't pay you even the lowest union rate. Your name is still dirt in the business because you outed your last costar. Joel Lowenstein would probably dredge all of that up again, overshadowing any mention of the actual show in his column." She finally looks at me. "Oh, wait. Let's don't forget the big reason—you're still a reckless party girl who puts herself in the position to be drugged by pranksters, dressed like a giant hot-dog, and driven around downtown in an even bigger hot dog." She falters, her eyes filling with tears before she looks away again. "You're just another scandal waiting to happen."

I grab her hands, but she still avoids my gaze. "I'm not. Yes, I went to that party because I was devastated that you ditched me and needed the ego boost I'd get from parading my acting success in front of my old high school bullies." My throat tightens around my next confession. "And Butch told me that Tommy and Bruce were coming over after the play. I was desperate to see Tommy and find out how the show was going." I pause. "No. That's not totally true. I needed to know if you were sad or happy to be free of me."

A few tears trickle down her cheeks as she meets my gaze again, and her throat works, but she doesn't speak.

"Please, Asia. I can do *Traditions* pro bono. Don't call off the show. The cast and volunteers have worked hard over the past few months, and they're depending on you. The entire town is depending on you and this theater to bring the tourists back. Plus, you owe it to yourself to let people see what a great play you've written and produced here."

She stares at me, then finally nods. "Okay."

I scoop her into my arms for a tight hug. "Thank you, thank you."

She steps back when I release her, hand on my chest to keep me at arm's length. "No. Thank you for saving our asses."

"I promise you won't regret this." I start backing toward the door. "I've got to go into the city for a meeting right now, but I'll be back for the two o'clock matinee. Rebecca's wardrobe should fit me fine."

"Davis."

I stop my turn to leave. "Yeah?"

"This doesn't change things between us. You're coming back for the role, not for us."

"I understand. See you this afternoon." Despite her warning, hope blooms in my chest. I emerge from the semidarkness of the auditorium into the sunlit lobby and dance my way over to my janitor friend. I grab his mop from his hands and do a quick Fred Astaire routine. "I'm back. Let me out. I've got things to do before the afternoon show."

CHAPTER NINETEEN

S o, they've sent a goddamn little-girl rookie to push me out to pasture. Isn't that a kick in the nuts."

I stare at the actor who is to play counterpoint to my character. "Well, from my point of view, I'm the one who's been kicked in the nuts. They've stuck me with a sour old man whose balls are probably hanging so low, I wouldn't know where to aim."

James Martin stares back at me. I'm thrilled at the chance to work with this consummate actor. His timing is impeccable. "I was going to point out that girls don't have balls, but it seems that you do."

"Woman. I quit being a girl when I turned nineteen and lost my virginity." I tap an imaginary shield hanging from my belt. "And I'm no rookie. I spent ten years on a street beat and earned this gold shield."

He scowls. "Rookie detective. Don't be expecting me to dry off your ears."

I lean in close so that our noses are almost touching. "Don't expect me to do all the reports and online research just because you refuse to learn how to use the computer system."

"Cut." Shelley, the casting director, smiles at us. "That was great, you guys. You definitely have the chemistry we're looking for. Thanks, James, for coming by this morning."

"No problem." He holds out his hand, which I accept with a warm handshake. "Good luck, kid." Then he waves a farewell and takes his leave.

"Let's talk about your availability," Shelley says to me.

"What's your timeline?" I ask.

"I know this is short notice, but we were hoping to start shooting right after the new year."

"Where?"

"We want to do some crossovers with Sandra's fire-station show, and that's filmed in Philadelphia."

"That works for me. I was hoping to work on the East Coast for a while. I have family close by, and I'm burned out on the LA scene."

"Just to be up front, we're aware of the problem that got you killed off your previous show."

I nod. "A mistake in judgment I won't ever make again." I pause before laying out my request. "I'm sure you'll understand, then, when I say that if I get this job, I don't want my character to get into a lesbian relationship."

"You're worried about being typecast because of your sexual orientation." Her statement sounded like a fact, not a question.

"Exactly."

"I think we can work with that." She sits back and smiles, slapping her hands together. "So, we'll call your agent and iron out the contract details."

I hold back a fist-pump because I'm trying desperately to maintain a cool, professional demeanor. "Yes, thank you. I'm excited to work on a Sandra Rawls production and at the prospect of acting with James. I've admired his work since I was a kid."

"Excellent." She begins to gather her notes and stuff them into a messenger bag. "We'll be in touch."

We walk out of the building together but separate when she hails a cab to the airport and I head down the street to the parking deck where my Jeep waits. Once her cab turns the corner out of sight, I leap into the air with an enthusiastic fist-pump. "Yes! I'm back!"

❖

The theater is far from full, but the audience stands and applauds us like they've just seen *Hamilton*. The old thrill I haven't experienced in years runs through me as the entire cast lines up for final bows. This is theater. This is immediate audience feedback you never experience while filming a television show or movie. It must be the high musicians ride during a successful live concert. And this is the second time today the crowd has honored us so enthusiastically. I'm elated.

Asia leaves the lighting and sound booth and slow-claps as she walks down the aisle to the stage while the audience is still cheering.

Trey and I each take one of her hands and lift her onto the stage with us. "Asia du Muir, ladies and gentlemen. Our playwright and producer."

They cheer even louder.

We're all breathless when the curtain is finally lowered and our audience begins to leave.

"Wow." Tommy's grinning like an idiot. "I'd forgotten how awesome it is to be on the stage with you."

I bump his shoulder. "Thanks, buddy. Everybody was really on it tonight. I had a few missteps, but I think I covered them well enough."

An enthusiastic Trey scoops me up and twirls me around before he puts me back down. "If you screwed up, I didn't notice," he says. "Your timing is so great...you're so easy to follow..." He stops as if to catch his breath and focus his thoughts. "I felt like I gave the best performance of my life because you made it so easy. You're coming back tomorrow, right?"

"Absolutely. I told Asia I'd fill in for as long as it takes to find another Rebecca and get her up to speed, or until the end of your run. There's only about three more weeks."

Our stage manager tugs at my elbow. "Asia wants you in the lobby. A big crowd's waiting to get your autograph."

I take Trey's hand and pull him along with us. "You too, buddy. You were great tonight, and that made my job much easier." I want to grab Asia, but she's in a deep conversation with a man wearing a priest's collar.

I expected a few autograph-seekers in the lobby, but a large crowd greets me. Trey and I sign programs and shirts and an assortment of weird items for more than thirty minutes before the crowd begins to thin. A guy who has been lingering on the edge of the mob finally steps forward.

"Hi, Ms. Hart. I'm Raleigh Johnson. I work as a freelance journalist and was wondering if I could set up an interview with you."

I stiffen. "I don't talk to internet bloggers."

His face reddens. "No, no. I don't blog. I mean, I do some blogging, but about journalism and what it's like to be a journalist today." He gives me a pointed stare. "I don't blog entertainment gossip. I write slice-of-America features and sell them to legitimate news outlets like the Associated Press, *USA Today*, the *Washington Post*, or the *New York Times Magazine*."

"How did you know I'd be here tonight?" I'm still suspicious of him.

"I didn't. I'm working up a feature on a town called Christmas, and everyone said the community theater was a big part of drawing in tourists, but it's been struggling since the pandemic. So I thought that would be a great news hook to sell the article."

His explanation makes sense, and an article in a major publication could help even more than a critic's review column that only theater enthusiasts are likely to read. Still, I hesitate.

"I can't make decisions for the show. Let me discuss it with Asia. *Traditions* is her show. And, honestly, I've had so much trouble with the West Coast paparazzi, I'm going to check you out to make sure you're published by legitimate media, not just some fly-by-night blogger trying to make money by playing on the internet."

"Please do." He gives me his business card. "Just so you know I'm not impersonating Raleigh Johnson—" He holds out his driver's license.

"Yep. That's you." I hand it back to him.

"I've sold articles to *USA Today* and the *New York Times Magazine* recently, if you want to call their features editors to check my references."

"Thanks." I examine his business card. "I'll do that."

"That's my mobile number on the card. You should be able to reach me anytime. If you do get my voice mail, I'll call you right back."

"Thank you. I'll be in touch." I turn away, only to come nose to nose with Trey.

"He wants to write an article about the show?" he asks. "That's so cool. It could really help ticket sales."

I shake my head. "Or draw a swarm of paparazzi."

❖

Joel Lowenstein looks pensive each time I glance discreetly his way...except once. Is that a smile? Yes, a small one, but definitely a smile at the banter between Rebecca and her maid. Jean's timing is spot-on as she bustles about trying to gather up the clothes I'm considering, then discarding on the floor, bed, and anywhere else on the set while I rant about my husband and in-laws.

The theater is nearly full for the Thursday-evening performance, and Joel rises with the rest for a standing ovation as we take our final bows. He doesn't applaud, but when his eyes meet mine, he gives a slight nod. That's good, right?

"He likes it," Tommy whispers as he takes another bow.

"Fingers crossed," I whisper back.

Again, we are summoned to the lobby to sign autographs, but Trey and I drag Tommy and several other members of the cast with us. I'm surprised to see one of our local merchants behind a folding table laden with T-shirts sporting the Chamber of Commerce's "I Love Christmas" logo and featuring a picturesque little town. People are lined up to buy them, then bring them over for the cast to autograph. I'm already thinking that we should design our own Christmas Community Theater T-shirts and sell them.

I feel a tug at my sleeve and turn around to find Mom, Al, Cora, and Joel.

"That was so wonderful, Davis," Mom says. "Asia's script was both funny and moving. I cried at the end."

"Oh, me, too." Cora holds up a monogrammed cloth. "Joel had to give me his handkerchief."

Joel holds out his hand for a brief handshake. "I was surprised when they announced before the curtain lifted that you'd be playing the role of Rebecca. This is a community theater, isn't it?"

"Yes. I'm the only pro. The others are either college students or long-time members of this theater troupe—people who live and work here in Christmas."

"You grew up here." It's a statement because his mother, as a friend of Mom, obviously has filled him in.

"In this town, and in this theater," I say.

"Why aren't you on the playbill?"

"I came to help my mom recover from back surgery, and after running into some of my old friends, talked Asia into letting me help coach some of the college students she was bringing in as part of her grant project. When we lost both the female lead and her understudy during the week we opened, I offered to stand in since I already knew the part."

"You seem very comfortable onstage," he says.

"My roots are in theater. I love the instant feedback from the audience. You don't get that in television or films."

"Do you have plans for Broadway?"

"I hope someday to work there. Right now, I have another television offer in the works. A very good one."

He shakes my hand again. "Good luck, then."

Tension flows out of my body like a cleansing breath. Critics are like the dragons of our industry. They can turn you into burned toast with a stroke of their pen. Who knew Joel would be a nice guy? I'm surprised when he stops and traces his steps back to me.

"Off the record, why aren't you on the playbill?"

I stare into his eyes. Can I trust him? After a long moment, I decide to be truthful.

"I love this quaint little place and everybody in it. I want to help the town and the people who are struggling to keep this theater alive. I don't want to bring a bunch of paparazzi down on their heads, digging up my Hollywood skeletons. This play is about reviving the town of Christmas, not my mistakes."

"Understood."

❖

My heart is still pounding from my climax when Asia rolls over, turning her back to me.

We'd had a few drinks backstage with the exuberant cast and crew after we revealed that critic Joel Lowenstein had been in the audience and appeared to like what he saw. Then, before I had time to rethink the situation, she was leading me up the stairs to her apartment.

Now the pleasure that had gripped my belly when her head was between my legs and her tongue on my clit is a cold ball of alarm. I follow her roll to press against her back, sweaty from our exertions. "Baby, what is it?"

Her shoulders hitch, and a choked sob comes from her beautiful mouth.

I kiss along her shoulder and stroke her arm to try to calm her. "Did I do something to hurt you?"

"Yes." Another sob. "No."

"Asia, honey, look at me and tell me what's wrong."

Slowly she rolls onto her back to face me. The sight of her tears makes my eyes water and my throat tighten. Her fingertips are a soft tickle along my cheek. "I can't...we can't do this."

"I don't understand." That cold ball in my belly is turning to ice. "Your play is a success. I'll bet my Jeep, currently my only real possession, that if Joel Lowenstein writes something in his column about us, it'll be good."

She nods, but tears still drip from the corners of her eyes.

I soften my voice. "We're good together, Asia." I hold back the three words I'm dying to say. "Why won't you give us a chance?"

She shifts her gaze away from me. "Because it'll never work." She briefly closes her eyes, and her tears stop. "I heard what you told Joel. You have another TV deal in the works. My life is here." She brings her gaze back to mine. "Your life, your career is in Hollywood."

I finally smile. "The people I'm talking with are planning to film in Philly. I'm not going anywhere very far."

"This time, Davis. Some TV shows don't last more than a season or two. What about the next TV offer you get? Or maybe it'll be a film opportunity. You know this type of marriage never works." She sits up and moves to get off the bed.

"Newman and Woodward. Kurt Russell and Goldie Hawn. Um, um, Rita Wilson and Tom Hanks. Sarah Jessica Parker and Matthew Broderick."

She's pulling on her robe, then picking up our clothes that are strewn across the floor. "A handful of couples among hundreds that lasted only a few years or a few months." She separates the clothes she's picked up and places mine next to me on the bed. "Please get dressed."

"You're throwing me out? It's the middle of the night."

She stares down at her feet. "I need to focus on myself and on my career. I don't have time to work on a relationship." She tosses my shoes at my feet.

"Asia."

She whips around, giving me her back again. "Just please leave." She opens the door to the bathroom. "And lock the door on your way out." With those final words, she walks into the bathroom and shuts the door. The lock clicking in place is a bullet to my heart.

CHAPTER TWENTY

The Friday and Saturday shows are torture. Asia and I barely speak, but I focus on my role onstage and turn in the best performances of my life. My pain becomes Rebecca's confusion over how to reconcile her own feelings and convictions with those of her parents and in-laws. Why can't they see things her way? Why should fears founded in the past rule Rebecca and Michael's future?

Al is over for Sunday brunch when I drag myself out of bed and shuffle into the kitchen wearing the boxer shorts and T-shirt I slept in.

"Davis, go put on some clothes. We have company." Mom is setting out plates while Al flips some delicious-smelling crepes.

I look around. "I don't see anybody but you and Al, and he's over here so much it's like he lives here."

"Davis!" Mom looks shocked, and Al turns to me, his brows raised.

I shake my head to wake up a little more. "No. That came out wrong. I meant to say, Al feels like another member of the family. I don't mind it at all, but if he's going to be over here a lot, he might as well get used to the horror that is me when I first get up."

Al laughs, and Mom gives me an affectionate shake of her head.

"I see scarier when I look in the mirror before I shave each morning," Al says. "My hair's sticking up in all directions."

That's hard to imagine because he's always immaculately groomed.

Mom touches my arm. "How are you doing, honey?"

"You mean since Asia dumped me, again?" Yeah. I'm bitter.

Before Mom can respond, the back door flings open, and Tommy runs into the kitchen without knocking.

"He reviewed us. It's in the Sunday paper." He holds up the entertainment section of the newspaper, folded into quarters, and then begins reading.

In a world that's so divided by religion, Asia du Muir has written a comedic yet thoughtful play called Traditions. *It's about Judaism, Christianity, and the approaching holidays.*

Rebecca and Trey are the non-religious parents of a very young son. When they return just before the holidays after living overseas for several years, they become caught up in the battling traditions of his Christian parents and her Jewish parents.

You can't see this show on or off Broadway. You must travel to the sleepy town of Christmas, Pennsylvania, where it's Christmas year-round. Directed and produced by Ms. du Muir, the play is presented by the Christmas Community Theater and the most outstanding volunteer troupe of actors I've ever witnessed. There's one volunteer actor, however, who shines the brightest.

Davis Hart was wasted as a television actress, because the real depth of her talent explodes onstage. Her acting expertise is rooted in theater, she told me, so it's easy to see why she appears so comfortable there.

It is community theater and produced, I understand, on a shoestring budget provided by a grant. So, while the sound system is good quality, the sets are a bit sparse, and the theater could use some updating. Regardless, the entertainment is well worth an hour-long drive from the city.

Make a day of it if you go to see the show. The town of Christmas is also one of the best places to shop for unique gifts, many made by local artisans.

The holidays never end for this small town, but the show does. You should go soon if you want to experience Ms. Hart's portrayal of Rebecca. Traditions will end when the new year rings in.

If you miss this production, do not despair. I predict there will be more notable theatric ventures by the talented playwright Ms. du Muir and by Ms. Hart.

"Wow," Mom says, her eyes wide. "Davis. That's an amazing review."

I'm a little stunned. No, a lot stunned. I'm speechless. Joel isn't known for gushing over plays. Like most critics, he tears apart as much as he builds up. Finally, I find my voice. "Does Asia know about this?"

"Call her," Tommy says. "You've got to call her."

I hesitate. "She might not want to talk to me."

"Not talk to the star of her show? You've got to be kidding." I haven't shared with Tommy that Asia threw me out of her bed, but he's not stupid and has surely noticed the tension between us. He's just discreet enough to let me tell him in my own time.

In my moment of indecision, my phone rings, and her name appears on the caller ID. I answer quickly. "Hey."

"Have you seen it? The Sunday paper? He likes it." She's practically squealing with exuberance.

"Tommy just busted in our back door to give us the news."

"I can't believe it. He called me a talented playwright."

"Because you are." I stop before I add *beautiful and brilliant and the woman who's breaking my heart.*

She pauses. "I couldn't have done this without your help."

"Nah. You'd have found a way. You're one of the most determined people I know." How grateful is she? Will she give us another chance? "Al's cooking crepes. Why don't you join us for brunch? Then we can go to the theater. I'm betting the rest of the cast will show up early, buzzing about the review."

She sighs audibly. "Thanks. I appreciate that, but I don't want to start any gossip by coming over to your house."

I shake my head to let Al know she's turned down my offer and leave the kitchen for this private part of our conversation. "What gossip? I'm offering brunch with a crowd of people—me, Mom, Al, and Tommy."

"Davis." She clears her throat. "What do you think the gossip bloggers will make it look like, me coming over to your mom's house? You were sleeping with your costar before. It will look like the same old Davis, this time sleeping with the play's producer. It won't help either of our careers."

"Who's going to know, Asia? Is the paparazzi standing outside your door already?" My hurt is turning into angry frustration. "Never mind. I'll see you at the theater for the matinee."

I stomp back into the kitchen and toss my phone onto the kitchen island. "She doesn't want to be seen with me outside the theater." Tommy, Mom, and Al stare at me. "She's afraid my bad reputation might hurt her career if people think we're sleeping together."

"But you are sleeping together." Tommy must want me to say it.

"Were." I spit the word out between my clenched teeth. "Were is the key word here. We were sleeping together, and then we weren't, and then we were. Now, we're not. She kicked me out of her bed Friday morning."

Tommy slumps in his seat but accepts the crepe Al places in front of him. "So, that's why you've been weird and so focused the past few days. I thought it was just some getting-into-character thing you picked up in Hollywood."

I want to rant about how unfair everything is, and eight months ago I would have. I dig into the crepe Al now shoves in front of me, just to fill my mouth so I won't say any more. For the first time in my life, I feel responsible for all of it. I knew I shouldn't sleep with my costar, who had a long reputation of being deeply closeted while going through girlfriends like ecstasy at a rave. And I knew better than to get publicly drunk and rant about her to a stranger. Now I also know not to accept a drink, alcoholic, or otherwise, from some guy at a party.

I don't, however, feel responsible for falling for Asia. I was drawn to her the first moment I saw her. Even the warning bells clanging in my head—danger, danger, stay clear of women—couldn't save me. Irresponsible? No. It was inevitable.

I swallow hard to get the delicious crepe past the lump in my throat. "She's right. That review is probably going to attract some of those gossip bloggers that have been trying to find me. If they sniffed even a hint that we were dating, they'd go after her."

"Oh, honey." Mom is sympathetic but doesn't disagree.

I push my plate away. "The food's great, Al. I'm just not very hungry. I think I'll go ahead and get in the shower." I leave the room and a very sympathetic silence.

❖

"Suck it up, suck it up." I pace and coach myself as I prepare to take the stage for Sunday's matinee. There are no dressing rooms in this small theater, just a line of four chairs in front of mirrors on a back wall, where we take turns for makeup and hair styling, and two screened-off areas for male and female costume changes. Today, I've managed to find a private space behind one of two large background sets that roll out into place for their scenes. A light knock on one of those sets stops me mid-pace.

"Are you okay, Davis?" Susan, my ex-girlfriend, stands at the end of one set in the semidarkness.

"Yeah, yeah. I'm okay." I know why she's asking. Acting

is a study in body language and how to use it to convey emotion and intent. Asia and I haven't had to say a thing for the rest of the cast to read what's been going on between us.

"I just wanted to say I'm sorry."

I begin to pace again, shaking my hands out at my sides. "Why are you sorry? I would think you'd be gloating. You have a right to. I'm finally reaping what I've sown."

She smiles but shakes her head. "I didn't know you've turned religious."

I give her a baleful glance.

"I know I was bitter and not very nice when you first showed up, but you've changed since you've been here."

I stop again and turn to her. "What do you mean?"

"When you were first back, you were still in poor-me mode. Nothing that happened out there was your fault. You acted like you expected to come East, and Broadway would greet you with open arms after success with one television show."

I hang my head. "You're right." My ego had been ridiculously oversized. I'm embarrassed at how I behaved.

She comes to me and grasps my hand. "But you're different with her, with Asia. Why is that?"

I shake my head. "I'm sorry, Susan. I really am. I knew you were more invested in us than I was, and it was shitty of me to leave without talking to you. I had blinders on. All I could see were stars...my big chance to be somebody, to be a real actor. I didn't think about you or Mom or Tommy...the people who cared about me, who I should have cared about."

"It's okay now. Your mom is doing great. Tommy is married and loves his teaching job." She smiles. "I'm ridiculously happy with Andie. We're a much better match than you and I ever were."

I squeeze her hand. "I'm happy for you. Really. She seems like a great person."

She squeezes my hand back and then lets go. "Everything's going to be okay, Davis. I feel it. So, keep that chin up, and break a leg tonight."

I wish I was as certain as she is. "Yeah. You break a leg, too."

The stage manager shouts a warning for everyone. "Five minutes to curtain. Five minutes."

Susan backs away. She's playing the role of Trey's mother, so we're both in the first scene. "Guess we better find our marks."

❖

"Who are you sleeping with in this show, Davis? Have you talked to Lisa Langston since you left LA?"

Even though I expected the paparazzi, the question shouted from the edge of the friendly autograph seekers still jolts me. I ignore it and finish signing the programs thrust at me after Sunday evening's sellout show.

Asia is a few feet away, also signing programs with Trey and me. She joined us only after several people asked for her. Someone has redesigned our playbill to list me in the role of Rebecca and include Joel's review that mentioned Asia as being on the rise in theater. I'm happy she's being recognized because *Traditions* truly is her work. Still, it stings that she walked around us to stand on the other side of Trey, distancing herself from me when she joined us.

A half hour later, the last of the excited fans leave, clutching signed playbills in their hands, but two men linger. I recognize the freelance journalist who'd approached me before, but not the other man, who's been snapping photos while we talked with fans.

"Isn't this little show a big step down from your role on *Judge and Jury?*" he asks as he pushes past the journalist. "Have you spoken with Lisa since they killed you off the show?"

I realize this must be the paparazzi who had shouted similar questions before. Before I can respond, Tommy comes through the doors of the auditorium with Bruce, who's still in uniform after his shift.

"The show's over, sir." Bruce steps between me and the two men. "Y'all need to leave the theater now so they can close up."

"Not him." I point to the journalist. "He has an appointment with us." I indicate the other man. "I don't know him, but he looks like the guy who's been stalking me." No one has been stalking me, of course, but I know the accusation will give Bruce some grounds for detaining him.

"I just got into town a few hours ago. I haven't been stalking anyone," the man says. "I'm just doing my job."

Bruce takes him by the arm. "How about coming with me and explaining yourself down at the station, where I can check out your story."

I mouth a "thank you" to Bruce, then gesture for the journalist to come meet our group. "Guys, this is Raleigh Johnson, who's legitimate. He approached me last week, and I've checked him out. Let's all go into to the office and talk."

Asia looks skeptical, and her tone holds a warning. "Davis."

"Trust me. Please?"

She gives me a look that I interpret as part sadness and part resignation, but she follows me without protest.

I explain that Raleigh is writing a piece on the town but wants to use the revival of this community theater as the news hook.

"I've already pitched this story to *USA Today* and the *Times* lifestyle editor. I won't lie. If you let me write it, I'll get a nice fee from the *Times*. They outbid the Gannett people."

Trey grins and fist-pumps, while Tommy covers his open mouth with his hand. They both look to Asia for her response.

Asia glances nervously at me, so I point to her messenger bag on the office's desk. "Get your laptop out and google him. He has several recent articles in *USA Today* and the *Washington Post*."

She's always thorough, so she does as I ask. We all wait anxiously as she scans the articles with his byline. Finally, she closes the laptop.

"I'll allow it with one condition."

Raleigh nods slowly. "What's that?"

"I want no mention of the scandal Davis was involved in out West."

He cocks his head and is silent for a minute. "I'll have to mention that she came home to Christmas after her role on *Judge and Jury* ended, but I can promise I won't bring up any speculation or rumors about why her character was killed off. To do so would only distract readers from the story I'm trying to write…an uplifting holiday feature about a community theater that will very possibly save Christmas. In addition to how this cast and crew came together, I'll be interviewing local merchants about how this theater is the heart of the town."

"Okay, then."

We all sigh in relief as Asia consents.

"It's late, though. I don't know about everyone else, but I'm wiped after two performances today," I say. "Why don't Asia, Trey, and I meet you at the coffee shop at ten tomorrow morning. Then you can interview any of the other cast members you want before tomorrow night's performance." I look to Asia. "Doesn't that sound okay?"

"Yes. And Tommy should join us, too. He can give you the background on the theater's struggle over the past few years."

"School hasn't let out for the holidays yet, but the music teacher can cover a couple of hours for me. Our classes are rehearsing together for our holiday extravaganza."

"Thanks," Asia says. "Then we'll meet up tomorrow." We start to file out of the office, but she calls to me. "Davis, can you stay a moment?"

Has she changed her mind? Does she want me, us back? I feel like a puppy that wants, needs to wiggle and leap into her arms for kisses, but instead I stop and wait obediently for her to speak and reveal her intentions.

"I need to thank you for everything you've done for the show, and for me."

"Asia." I take a step toward her, but she holds up a hand.

"I don't want you to feel that I don't appreciate it, whatever your motive might be."

"My motive? I just want the show, and you, to be a success. You deserve it."

She finally smiles. "The jury is still out on my career, but *Traditions* is a success. And you may have almost single-handedly saved the town of Christmas. So, thank you."

"Can I get a kiss for that?"

She shakes her head, her eyes filling.

"How about a hug?"

"No. Please don't make this harder than it is." She speaks in a choked whisper.

Ignoring her request, I take her hands. "Relationships are hard, sweetheart. They take work. Can't we try?"

She yanks her hands out of mine. "No, Davis. No. We'll say that we'll try, but then one of us will be offered the project of a lifetime, and she'll take it, no matter how many hundreds of miles away or for how many months we'll be separated. Then we'll drift apart, and one of us will cheat, and the hurt will be ten times worse than if we just stop what's happening between us right now."

I shake my head and stand my ground. "I've never thought you were a coward."

"Then you misjudged me." She skirts around me, pausing in the doorway. "You are my colleague, one who has gone above and beyond to make this show a success. I'll see you at the coffeehouse in the morning."

And then she's gone.

CHAPTER TWENTY-ONE

We have three more weeks and more than thirty afternoon and evening performances until our last scheduled show on the eve of New Year's Day. It's a tough schedule, even for paid actors, and a huge ask of volunteers. Even though filming a television series can mean long, grueling days, we almost always have weekends off and new scenes to shoot each day. In the end, it doesn't compare to the grind of presenting the same script, sometimes twice, day in and day out. It takes a special kind of dedication to keep each performance fresh and enthusiastic.

I'm lying prone on my bed, staring at the ceiling to give myself a pep talk, when my phone begins to sing "Who let the dogs out?"

"Hey, Kylie. What's up?"

"The Sandra Rawls people want to meet with you again about *District 12*. They've made some pretty big changes in what they pitched to you before. I think you need to talk to them before I draw up a contract."

"What sort of changes?"

"I don't know all the details, but it sounds like they want to shift the filming location. I know you want to stay on the East Coast, but this is a great opportunity for you. If the series is successful, this could be your signature role."

"That's a big if."

"When have you ever heard of a Sandra Rawls project flopping?"

"Well, never, but she must have had some early flops."

"Why are you being so negative today?"

"I don't know." But I do know. Why won't Asia give us a chance? I can't stop thinking about her, missing her. "Ignore me. I suspect the reality of true theater has just sunk in. How do some actors do the same show week in and week out for years and still make each performance seem fresh?"

"You grew up acting in that same theater. Their plays always ran for months before another one began."

"Yeah, but we usually had dual casts, so nobody had to do every performance. We had to because we all had regular lives outside the theater. Kids had school, and most of the adults had full-time jobs."

"What's really bothering you?"

"Honestly? I don't really know. Maybe I'm coming down with something."

"Well, put a hold on that. The theater is closed on Mondays, right? So, you're free today?"

"I have a meeting at ten with a journalist who's doing a feature on the theater and the town. A group of us are meeting with him."

"The guy you asked me to have checked out?"

"Yeah. That's him."

"Then you can go to the city to meet with the Rawls people this afternoon?"

"Sure."

"I'll set the meeting up for three o'clock. Same offices."

"Okay. I'll be there."

"Davis."

"What?"

"Have you even thought about the off-Broadway show Phil mentioned to you? I hear they're still looking for the right person to play the lead."

"The lesbian thing? Not really. He said it was from a comic strip."

"Yeah. *Jane's World*. I've been a fan for years. The artist is a professional cartoonist and an executive with the Charles Schultz organization."

"You mean like Snoopy and Charlie Brown?"

"Yeah. But she's also the author of a handful of children's books, as well as some lesbian romances she writes under a pen name. But this play is based on a novel she wrote that includes her comic-strip characters. It's about Jane, a cute but sort of naive lesbian, whose PayBuddy account is hacked, and the hacker buys a mail-order bride who shows up on Jane's doorstep one day. It's hilarious material that I'm betting will be as big a hit as Alison Bechdel's *Fun Home*."

"I'm worried about playing a lesbian role, given my problems in LA."

"I understand. But you should think about this one. It won't pay nearly as much or draw the audience the television series would, but you need to decide which project will make you the happiest. Until today, you've seemed a lot happier than the party girl you were in California. Just saying. Think about it."

"Yeah. Okay. But I have to go now if I'm going to make that meeting."

"Let me know what you decide."

"I will." I pause. "Thanks, Kylie. Thanks for so many things, but especially for being my friend."

"Always, buddy."

❖

Raleigh spends equal time interviewing Tommy about the struggles of the Christmas Community Theater and its connection with the town's economic health, Asia about writing the play and securing the grant to produce it, and me about how my connection to the town landed me back in the theater where I developed my acting chops. He even briefly asks Trey about how he became involved and his career expectations beyond our show.

Tommy's and Trey's answers to his questions are just background noise, because the only voice I'm listening to, the only responses I'm watching, are Asia's. Damn, she's gorgeous. Not in a magazine-model kind of way, but in a natural-beauty way. I could look at her lovely face all day as she listens, and pauses, and responds. She's the air I want to breathe, the sustenance I need to keep me living rather than existing.

"Davis?" Tommy nudges me under the table with his foot. "Earth to Davis."

"Uh, what? I'm sorry. I was thinking about a meeting I have later today in the city."

"I asked if you've decided on your next project after this," Raleigh says.

"Oh." I stare at my hands for a few seconds. "I was talking with my agent this morning about two very different offers I have on the table, but I haven't decided which I'll pursue yet."

"Theater, television, or film?" he asks.

"I'd rather not say at this point. I don't know whether either of the projects has been made public yet."

Raleigh glances at his watch. "Thanks, you guys. If I have any more questions once I start writing, I'll give Asia a call."

"Do you know when it will be published?" Trey asks for all of us.

"The editor has targeted it for Thursday's lifestyle-section cover. So I have to start writing today. They'll probably send a photographer around tomorrow. Is that okay?"

Asia nods. "Sure. Tell him or her to ask for me when they come to the theater."

We say our good-byes, and I head down the street to where I'm parked.

"Two offers?"

I whirl around, not having realized Asia has followed me. "Uh, yeah."

"Are you going to run off and leave me high and dry before our show ends?"

"No. Never. You can't get rid of me that easy."

Her shoulders visibly relax. "Are you excited about these offers?"

"Both are incredible projects, but very different. I don't have the details yet on either, but it's going to be a tough decision."

She studies me for a long moment, searching my eyes. I know she must see my longing for her. Then she takes my hand in her warm ones. "Go with your heart, Davis. Don't look at money, or what others think you should do, or doors that could be opened in the future. Go with your heart. I want you to be happy."

I nod because my throat's too tight to produce words. She squeezes my hand, then turns back to unchain her bicycle and ride away.

❖

Shelley, casting director for Sandra Rawls, stands to greet me. "Good to see you again, Davis."

I shake her hand. "Thanks. I understand some things have changed from our first conversation."

"Yes." She gestures for us to sit. "You still are our first choice. Your reading with James Martin was exactly what we envisioned, and he agrees that you should be at the top of the list. The chemistry between you two is the kind of stuff that makes a memorable costar team. But I think location was a concern for you. We will be doing some filming in Philly, but, after looking at some budgeting concerns, the producers decided we can save a significant amount of money by filming most of it on sets in LA."

"So, how much time do you anticipate filming in LA?"

"We figure nine months to film twenty episodes, with at least six of those nine months in LA."

My heart drops. I really want this project, but I'm filled with fear of spending six months or more in Hollywood. Accepting this job would be giving up on Asia, and I haven't done that yet. I can still feel the spark between us, see in her eyes the connection that she's refusing still exists. Also, going back to the scene of my previous life feels like a reformed addict moving back into his old neighborhood, with dealers on every corner and dropping by his house.

"When do you have to know my decision?"

Shelley shifts uncomfortably. "We've already hacked out a contract with your agent—she drives a hard bargain, by the way—so all we need is your commitment. And I'm afraid I need it today. If you turn me down, I'll be meeting with our second choice this afternoon."

I stand and walk to the windows of the conference room to stare out. Signing on with this show would be a great come-uppance to flaunt before Lisa Langston and the *Judge and Jury* producers. But for some reason, those people just don't seem that important to me anymore. And six months in LA? I don't know why, but the very thought of it makes me want to throw up. I turn back to Shelley. "I'm sorry. I can't." I hold out my hand to her. "Good luck. I hope turning you down now doesn't mean I won't be considered for future Sandra Rawls shows. I have a lot of respect for her. I just have some personal reasons for really needing to stay on the East Coast right now."

"I understand. I loved your reading. Maybe we'll convince you to join another of our productions in the future."

"I hope so."

❖

"What have I done? Oh, my God. What have I done? Have I completely lost my mind?"

I'm halfway back to Christmas when panic sets in. My self-recrimination isn't enough. I need someone else to tell me how stupid I am.

"Siri, call Kylie."

"You turned them down?"

Wow. That was quick.

"No hello?"

"Okay. Hello, Davis. You turned them down?"

"Did they call you already? I'm not even home yet."

"No. I just had a feeling that's what you were going to do."

"I can't go back to LA. Not yet. I'm not that person anymore, but I'm afraid I will be if I live there again too soon." I realize this truth as I put words to the fear churning my belly.

She's quiet for a minute. "I am so proud of you for recognizing, and resisting, that temptation. I know it was hard. It could have been the role of a lifetime, but I have a feeling more opportunities will come your way."

"From your lips to God's ear, like Phil would say."

She laughs. "He's quite a character, and the best mentor I could have." She pauses. "Are you planning to consider that off-Broadway role he found for you?"

"Yeah. He's my next call."

"Good. You're perfect for it. I met with the author, Paige Braddock. She works at the Snoopy headquarters in Santa Rosa. It's really beautiful country up there. Not like the city here."

I hesitate. "We'll both make a whole lot less cash off-Broadway than we would have with the television series."

"Don't sweat the money. I've made plenty of commission off you over the past five years, and I do have other lucrative clients. Just know you'll get plenty of professional recognition, but you won't have near the public exposure you get from television."

"I actually wouldn't mind a little less public recognition. I'd like to go out to a restaurant without having my meal interrupted to sign autographs. And I'm sick of stupid, self-appointed bloggers and paparazzi."

"Is your fear of becoming a self-involved party girl again your only reason for turning the Rawls project down?"

"No." I answer quickly but pause to choose my next words carefully. "I'm not giving up on Asia. I know she wants us as much as I do, but she doesn't trust that we can make it work, considering both of our careers are project-driven and could mean months of separation. Few long-distance relationships survive after a time."

"Is it that she doesn't trust you, or that she doesn't trust herself?"

I think this over. "I don't know. All I know is that I want to try."

"Then you should go get your girl and sign up for the theater project." Two beeps interrupt her words. "I've got another call coming in. For what it's worth, I think you're on the right road, buddy. Now hang up and call Phil."

I laugh. "Catch you later."

CHAPTER TWENTY-TWO

You have to admit the Christmas Community Theater isn't typical since it used to be year-round. Don't most community troupes produce only one or two plays a year? Aren't most just groups of wannabe actors?"

"I'd like to answer those questions." I immediately jump in to tackle the student's haughty queries.

I'm at Columbia University, where, after the *New York Times* feature piece was published, Trey's acting professor invited Tommy and me to join Trey on a panel exploring the value of community theaters.

"The community theater groups range from very amateur to near-professional quality, depending on their financial support and the pool of actors they have to draw on. Some in smaller towns might be a group of people who are just having fun, while others in larger cities have the financial backing and professional guidance to nearly duplicate the Broadway acting experience."

Trey interrupts. "Even at the community level, acting in a play is a lot of hard work. We have to audition and then show up every day, sometimes twice a day, to rehearse. It's grueling." He grins at our audience. "The only difference from professional theater is that even the starring actors have to help put the sets and other equipment away before we all go home."

Tommy and I both chuckle at his comment.

"The Christmas troupe is more experienced than the average community theater group, but there are others just as strong, and some of their actors have gone on to successful careers in the field," Tommy says.

"Like who?" The question sounds more like a challenge than a query.

"Like Julia Roberts, whose parents created the Atlanta Actors and Writers Workshop in Atlanta during the 1960s," I say. "Also, Evan Rachel Wood, a star in the HBO series *Westworld*. She grew up acting with the Raleigh, North Carolina, community troupe, alongside her father Ira and her brother David."

A female student stares at me, then tentatively lifts her hand to be recognized. I nod my permission for her to speak.

"Have you ever considered doing something other than acting? I mean, doesn't it get old traveling from project to project all over the world?"

"I enjoy teaching and coaching actors, so that could be down the road for me. For now, I want to act, but that's not my top priority." I pause to collect my thoughts. I don't want these kids to become the selfish, self-centered person I became during my chase for fame and money. I find Asia in the shadows of the top-tier seating, leaning forward and tucking her hair behind her ears as though it might keep her from hearing my response. She'd turned down a place on our panel because she'll always prefer to write the script or direct rather than take the stage. "Honestly, I was a bit adrift after my character was killed off *Judge and Jury*, but coming home reminded me that family and good friends are more important than anything acting could give me."

❖

Ticket sales have soared after Raleigh's article appeared in the *Times*, and we're performing before sold-out crowds at almost every show, two shows a day since school has let out. Downtown Christmas is bloated with tourists, and I feel almost as full with the news that I've held back until I signed my contract this morning.

It's Christmas Eve, so we've held only a matinee, since shops are closing early and people are rushing home for family gatherings. We've been blessed with a long stretch of cold weather and snow flurries over the past few days, so spirits are high as the cast and crew lock everything down and leave amid cheery calls of "Happy holidays" and "Merry Christmas."

I wait while Asia locks the glass doors of the theater, then grab her hand. "Come with me? I have something for you." I'm pretty sure she'll do what I ask because she's been in an exceptionally good mood the past few days.

"Okay," she says. "I have something I want to share with you, too."

We climb into my Jeep, and I drive to our spot by the pond. She willingly takes my hand as we wind through the copse of snow-dusted firs to reach our bench. I've come prepared with a towel to dry our seat and a large umbrella, because the snow is growing from an occasional flake to a swirling flurry.

"You share first," she says.

"No. You first."

She grins the biggest smile I've ever seen from her. "I've accepted an offer to write for a new TV sitcom, starting in January." Her words are rushed and excited. "It's not theater, but the pay is pretty good for being part of a five-writer team, and it has pretty regular hours, so I will still have time to work up my next theater project."

My heart sinks as I force a smile. "Congratulations." Despite my best effort, I know she can hear the disappointment in my voice. "I guess you'll be heading out to LA, then." I just signed a contract to stay on the East Coast, but she's leaving? I start to babble while I try to digest this new development. "It's tough to find affordable housing out there, but I still have an apartment in Hollywood and just booted my subletter out. You could sublet from me if you like it, because"—my rush of words trails off to a whisper—"because I just signed a contract to play the lead in an off-Broadway production." I choke out the last words. "I'll be working in the city for as long as the show's successful."

Her eyebrows shoot skyward. "Really? Davis. That's fantastic."

"I thought so, too, until you just told me you'll be working in television out West, while I'll be here. I didn't tell you before, but I turned down an incredible TV role before I accepted the theater job."

She looks incredulous. "Why would you do that?"

I have to glance away from her because my stupid eyes are filling with tears. "Because I wanted to stay here. I wanted to talk you into giving us a chance." Tears are wetting my cheeks now. I feel like a fool.

She takes my face in her hands, forcing me to face her. "I'm not going to LA, silly. This show is filming in New York."

I fling myself at her, dropping the umbrella and burying my face in her shoulder so she can't see me ugly-cry. "I want…I want us to try. You make me feel things I've never felt for another woman. I want to be a better person for you."

She wraps her arms around me and strokes my hair. "Oh, honey. You've always been a good person under that Hollywood ego. Since that first time I met you in the coffeehouse, I've watched you peel away that cocky, strutting celebrity image you'd wrapped yourself in to uncover a thoughtful, loyal woman." She pulls out a fresh tissue she has folded in her pocket and puts it in my hand. "Getting to know you these past few months has been like unwrapping a Christmas gift."

I wipe my eyes and nose, but keep my head on her shoulder. I'm feeling shy about my next confession. "I love you, Asia. I've been in love with you for months now."

She pushes me back and lifts my chin so I'll meet her gaze. "I'm hopelessly in love with you, too. I'm tired of trying to convince myself that I'm not."

We share smiles for a very long minute before she glances

over at the utility box. The Out of Order sign is gone. "It's Christmas Eve. Don't you think we should send Santa on his way?"

"Yes!" I pull out my phone and open the app. After a bit of whirring and gears grinding, Rudolph with his red nose bursts from the woods, leading his team and Santa's sleigh over the pond and into the woods on the other side.

Asia claps like a child. "Again."

The snow is growing heavier, but I activate the app again and cuddle her in my arms while we watch Santa make a return trip with pristine white flakes swirling around him and his reindeer. When they disappear again into the woods, I imagine them rising above the trees in the distance, heading off to a long night of distributing toys.

We stand to leave, but I turn Asia to face me and kiss her with all the love and heat I can muster. "If you invite me home with you, I'll let you literally unwrap me. And I promise to be a very good present."

EPILOGUE

Six Months Later

Asia runs her fingers through my shortened hair. "I love this hairstyle. It looks so good on you." She plays with the short hair on the back of my head.

"I kind of like it, too. Cutting seemed a better option than tucking my hair up under a wig for every show."

We lie in our bed, naked and basking in the afterglow of an extremely successful opening night of *Jane's World: The Case of the Mail Order Bride*, followed by hot, passionate sex, then waking up in each other's arms.

"You are so perfect in that role," she says.

"The script is so much better since you fixed it. Paige said she's really glad they hired you. She wasn't happy with the first playwright's version."

"Paige Braddock is a totally nice person, and easy to work with professionally. It's her story, so she has a right to be satisfied that the theater version holds true to the book."

I sigh my contentment, entranced by her soothing strokes, and mumble an unconscious decision. "I want to spend the rest of my life with you."

Her hand stills. "Is that a campaign promise or a proposal?"

I blink out of my sleepy state. "Campaign promise?"

"Something proclaimed in the moment but unlikely to happen."

I sit up. "Neither. It's a heartfelt desire. But when I propose, you can expect romance, wine, candles, and maybe a flash mob." It seems I can make good decisions, even when I'm naked.

She pulls me down into the bedding again. "Come back here. I don't know what you set the air conditioner on, but I'm freezing. I need you to keep me warm."

"I set the temperature to cuddle," I say, happily wrapping myself around the best present Christmas has ever given me.

About the Author

D. Jackson Leigh grew up barefoot and happy, swimming in farm ponds and riding rude ponies in rural Georgia. She has retired from her career as a journalist, but continues her real passion—writing sultry lesbian romances laced with her trademark Southern humor and affection for dogs and horses.

She has published 18 novels and one collection of short stories with Bold Strokes Books, winning five Golden Crown Literary Society awards in paranormal, romance, and fantasy categories. She was also a finalist in the romance category of the 2014 Lambda Literary Awards.

You can friend her at facebook.com/d.jackson.leigh.

Books Available From Bold Strokes Books

Accidentally in Love by Kimberly Cooper Griffin. Nic and Lee have good reasons for keeping their distance. So why does their growing attraction seem more like a love-hate relationship? (978-1-63679-759-5)

Frosted by the Girl Next Door by Aurora Rey and Jaime Clevenger. When heartbroken Casey Stevens opens a sex shop next door to uptight cupcake baker Tara McCoy, things get a little frosty. (978-1-63679-723-6)

Ghost of the Heart by Catherine Friend. Being possessed by a ghost was not on Gwen's bucket list, but she must admit that ghosts might be real, and one is obviously trying to send her a message. (978-1-63555-112-9)

Hot Honey Love by Nan Campbell. When chef Stef Lombardozzi puts her cooking career into the hands of filmmaker Mallory Radowski—the pickiest eater alive—she doesn't anticipate how hard she'll fall for her. (978-1-63679-743-4)

London by Patricia Evans. Jaq's and Bronwyn's lives become entwined as dangerous secrets emerge and Bronwyn's seemingly perfect life starts to unravel. (978-1-63679-778-6)

This Christmas by Georgia Beers. When Sam's grandmother rigs the Christmas parade to make Sam and Keegan queen and queen, sparks fly, but they can't forget the Big Embarrassing Thing that makes romance a total nope. (978-1-63679-729-8)

Unwrapped by D. Jackson Leigh. Asia du Muir is not going to let some party-girl actress ruin her best chance to get noticed by a Broadway critic. Everyone knows you should never mix business and pleasure. (978-1-63679-667-3)

The First Kiss by Patricia Evans. As the intrigue surrounding her latest case spins dangerously out of control, military police detective Parker

Haven must choose between her career and the woman she's falling in love with. (978-1-63679-775-5)

Language Lessons by Sage Donnell. Grace and Lenka never expected to fall in love. Is home really where the heart is if it means giving up your dreams? (978-1-63679-725-0)

New Horizons by Shia Woods. When Quinn Collins meets Alex Anders, Horizon Theater's enigmatic managing director, a passionate connection ignites, but amidst the complex backdrop of theater politics, their budding romance faces a formidable challenge. (978-1-63679-683-3)

Scrambled: A Tuesday Night Book Club Mystery by Jaime Maddox. Avery Hutchins makes a discovery about her father's death that will force her to face an impossible choice between doing what is right and finally finding a way to regain a part of herself she had lost. (978-1-63679-703-8)

Stolen Hearts by Michele Castleman. Finding the thief who stole a precious heirloom will become Ella's first move in a dangerous game of wits that exposes family secrets and could lead to her family's financial ruin. (978-1-63679-733-5)

Synchronicity by J.J. Hale. Dance, destiny, and undeniable passion collide at a summer camp as Haley and Cal navigate a love story that intertwines past scars with present desires. (978-1-63679-677-2)

Wild Fire by Radclyffe & Julie Cannon. When Olivia returns to the Red Sky Ranch, Riley's carefully crafted safe world goes up in flames. Can they take a risk and cross the fire line to find love? (978-1-63679-727-4)

Writ of Love by Cassidy Crane. Kelly and Jillian struggle to navigate the ruthless battleground of Big Law, grappling with desire, ambition, and the thin line between success and surrender. (978-1-63679-738-0)